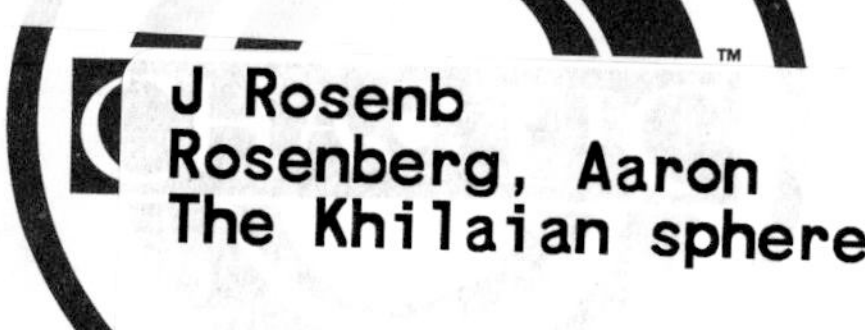

The M'arrillian Chronicles:

The Khilaian Sphere

GROSSET & DUNLAP
Published by the Penguin Group
Penguin Group (USA) Inc., 375 Hudson Street, New York, New York 10014, USA
Penguin Group (Canada), 90 Eglinton Avenue East, Suite 700,
Toronto, Ontario M4P 2Y3, Canada (a division of Pearson Penguin Canada Inc.)
Penguin Books Ltd., 80 Strand, London WC2R 0RL, England
Penguin Group Ireland, 25 St. Stephen's Green, Dublin
2, Ireland (a division of Penguin Books Ltd.)
Penguin Group (Australia), 250 Camberwell Road, Camberwell, Victoria
3124, Australia (a division of Pearson Australia Group Pty. Ltd.)
Penguin Books India Pvt. Ltd., 11 Community Centre,
Panchsheel Park, New Delhi—110 017, India
Penguin Group (NZ), 67 Apollo Drive, Rosedale, North Shore
0632, New Zealand (a division of Pearson New Zealand Ltd.)
Penguin Books (South Africa) (Pty.) Ltd., 24 Sturdee
Avenue, Rosebank, Johannesburg 2196, South Africa

Penguin Books Ltd., Registered Offices: 80 Strand, London WC2R 0RL, England

Published by Grosset & Dunlap, a division of Penguin Young Readers Group, 345 Hudson Street, New York, New York 10014. GROSSET & DUNLAP is a trademark of Penguin Group (USA) Inc. Printed in the U.S.A.

Library of Congress Control Number: 2009053388

ISBN 978-0-448-45400-9 10 9 8 7 6 5 4 3 2 1

CHAOTIC™
THE M'ARRILLIAN CHRONICLES
The Khilaian Sphere

Prologue

"It's working!" Chaor bellowed. "Aa'une's getting weaker! Don't let up!" He continued to attack, slamming the M'arrillian leader with gouts of fiery Energy. Chaor had tapped into ancient Mugic for this battle, and his changed appearance reflected that—the UnderWorld ruler was even taller and more powerfully built than ever, his red skin turned such a deep crimson it was almost black, and molten magma burned in the cracks that decorated his chest, back, and arms.

Maxxor growled but didn't say anything else as he lent his own formidable strength to the onslaught. The golden armor he wore shone in the light, the leonine helmet giving him a more ferocious appearance, though his own emerald skin was visible within its mouth and along his exposed arms and legs. He was one of the most powerful warriors in Perim, and the OverWorld leader, capable of defeating almost any foe . . .

. . . except perhaps the one that writhed before them, enduring their combined blasts.

Aa'une, the oligarch of the M'arrillians, towered above them. He had expanded into this powerful body upon their reaching Lake Blakeer, its energies feeding his own powerful psionics and granting him amazing new Power. His blue skin and glowing eyes still revealed his underwater origins as he thrashed about, attempting to evade the Symmetry Slam from Maxxor, Chaor, and their ally Iparu.

For a second, it looked as if the Attack had succeeded.

Then Aa'une roared in pain, fury—and something else. Something more like—exultation? His eyes flared with light, and then his body began to change a second time.

His foes watched in horror as Aa'une transformed even further. Long, black spikes sprouted from his back. His neck elongated, his head changing shape and becoming more snakelike. His body widened at the base, and long tentacles emerged on all sides. Then the folds in front shifted, and a second, hideous head sprouted from his chest. When the process was complete, he reared up to his full height. He resembled nothing so much as a monstrous octopus with a vicious eel mounted on top and a third mouth snapping from the middle.

"You were right, Maxxor!" the hideous Aa'une roared. "Your enemies aren't always what they appear to be! All this time I have been waiting to reveal my true form, and unleash my true Power. Psybercannon!" A beam of pure Power burst from the glowing protrusion in his forehead and lanced down at them.

Maxxor, Chaor, and Iparu dove out of the way. The Energy struck the ground instead, shattering it. Rocks flew as the entire surface of the floating island shifted and tore apart. Maxxor and Chaor barely managed to cling to pieces to avoid falling into Lake Blakeer below them. If they touched the deadly Energy-filled waters of the lake, it would mean instant destruction.

Iparu had reacted more quickly, and had gained stable ground right beside Aa'une. "Cyclone of Pain!" he shouted as he blasted the M'arrillian oligarch. Aa'une howled in agony and lashed out with a tentacle, snatching Iparu and squeezing him tight. Now it was Iparu's turn to scream in pain.

Out of desperation, Iparu began to reshape his body. His glowing blue-white form contracted, roiling about, and then darkened and expanded. It burst from Aa'une's grip and continued to billow and unfold. A head appeared. Then another. Then limbs and tentacles, and at last a long, sinuous neck. Iparu bellowed, and Maxxor and Chaor gaped. Their ally had transformed into—Aa'une!

The two massive Creatures launched themselves at each other. A burst of crimson Energy shot from Iparu's altered head, to be met by an icy beam from Aa'une. The two struggled, their beams swaying back and forth, but neither could gain an advantage.

"Iparu can't win!" Chaor declared as he and Maxxor watched the exchange. "We have to figure out a way to destroy Aa'une!"

Maxxor glanced around. It was just the four of them on the rock, so there was nowhere to turn for help. Then his eyes fell upon the dark waters raging around them. "All that Energy in Lake Blakeer is negatively charged," he pointed out. "If we hit Aa'une with an Attack that's positively charged and force him into the lake—"

"Let's do it!" Chaor agreed. He started forward.

"But which one's the real Aa'une?" The two monsters had twisted and lunged at each other, and now it was impossible to tell which was which.

Chaor shrugged and raised his arm. "Blast them both!"

But Maxxor grabbed the UnderWorld ruler's wrist and stopped him. "We can't destroy Iparu!" he insisted.

Chaor growled and shook his hand free, but didn't

argue. Instead he turned toward the battling pair. "Iparu!" he shouted. Then he made a mighty jump—right off the rock!

One of the monsters reacted immediately. It spun and swept out a tentacle, catching Chaor just before he fell into the lake's black waters.

Maxxor grinned. Clearly that was Iparu. He targeted the other—the real Aa'une—and blasted him.

"We have to force Aa'une into the lake," Chaor explained to Iparu as the shape-shifter set him down safely. "Hit him with another Symmetry Slam!"

All three of them attacked at once. Aa'une tried to resist, but their combined Power forced him back first one step, then another. Then his rearmost tentacle slipped off the rock. He tumbled backward, unable to right himself or latch on to anything, and plummeted down—and into the lake.

The second Aa'une's body struck the water, a crackle of Energy arced upward. A corresponding change raced across Lake Blakeer's surface, transforming the deadly waters into ice. All of that Energy had been turned inward, focused upon Aa'une. The M'arrillian leader was no more.

Gazing down at the frozen waters, Maxxor and Chaor shared a triumphant glance. They'd done it! The

M'arrillian Invasion was over! Working together, the other four Tribes had saved Perim!

Chapter One

Centuries earlier . . .

"Unbelievable!"

Varakarr stopped and straightened, tail quivering, and gaped at the vista that stretched out before him. Beside him, his mentor Khilai leaned on her staff and smiled.

"Yes, it is impressive, isn't it?" she asked him softly. They stood together near the edge of Lake Ken-I-Po. The mountains swept upward all around them, and that alone was reason enough to be amazed. Varakarr had never seen such heights, or felt the crisp cold that dwelled here high above the world, making him shiver despite the heavy robes he had donned for the occasion. Like all Mipedians, he was a Creature of the desert. His home was among the sand, where the sun baked all that it touched, or in the swamps along its edges, where the heat made the very air shimmer. Cold was new to him, and every scale ached from it—the horn rising from his snout was almost numb, as were the larger horns that swept back from his skull, and the ridge that rose between his eyes and continued down his back.

Khilai seemed less affected, the double crest atop her head still a vibrant red-gold instead of his own frozen dull orange, her eyes still sharp and bright beneath her cowl. But she had been here many times before, of course. As the High Mugess, it was her responsibility to travel here each turn of the moon. Here she met with her peers, and they discussed the world and their Tribes, seeking to resolve differences and maintain the balance. This was the first time she had chosen to bring Varakarr with her, however, though he had been her apprentice for many years already. And Varakarr knew he had every right to be astounded and awed by the mountains around them, and the glistening lake that lay before them.

Yet, grand as it was, the icy landscape had not been the reason for his exclamation.

No, his awe had been reserved for the sight of their destination. He had gasped, certainly, when he'd first spied the peaks, and again when he had caught a glimpse of the mirror-bright lake. But it was the vision of the majestic Citadel floating above the valley nearby, its four towers gleaming in the sunlight, that had made him give voice to his awe.

And, though she would never voice it, Varakarr suspected from her tone that Khilai privately agreed. Kaizeph, the ancient Citadel of the Elements, was a sight well worth gasps and shouts. How could it fail to make her heart sing and her blood race every time she beheld it? The noble city on its floating isle hovered there, some hundred body-lengths off the ground, unsupported by anything but its own magic. It was the oldest, grandest, most powerful structure in all of Perim, and all four Tribes revered it equally.

Khilai allowed him another minute to drink in the view before finally nudging him gently with her staff. "It's just as amazing close up," she told him with a chuckle. "But we won't ever know that if you stay here with your mouth open!"

"Oh? Oh! Yes, yes, of course!" Varakarr's jaw snapped shut and he rubbed at his crest with good-natured embarrassment. "Sorry, High Mugess."

She waved his apology aside. "Do not worry about it. But we really should be going. My counterparts do not like to be kept waiting."

Khilai set off at a brisk pace around the lake, and

Varakarr hurried to catch up with her. The cold seemed to billow from Lake Ken-I-Po's still surface, and even with their thick robes bundled about them both Mipedians shivered. *Why couldn't the city float above one of Perim's many deserts?* Varakarr wondered for the hundredth time since they'd left their own home city. *Or a nice, muggy swamp? Or jungle? Or even one of the temperate plains? Why did it have to be up here among all this ice and snow?*

Well, he chided himself, it was what it was. There was no changing Kaizeph. And for that he was grateful. It hovered here, separate from the usual fighting that tore at Perim, free from the strife between the Tribes. No one could claim it as part of their territory, which made it safe for all. He shuddered at the thought of any one Tribe, even his own, holding total power over Kaizeph—and the wellsprings it contained. That would be a disaster, no question. No, it was better for the floating city to remain here apart from all that, where the High Muges could meet in peace.

At last they reached the mouth of the valley, and left the lake behind as they began the last part of their trek. It had taken them several days to reach the mountains, and even that would have been many times longer if not for their Mugic, the musical magic they and the other Muges wielded. And that was another reason why Kaizeph floated here, at the top of the world. No one came here without a clear reason, for the journey was arduous for anyone. That kept the city safe from prying eyes and greedy hands, well away from the curious and the power-hungry.

Not that any of them would be able to reach it even if they could get here, Varakarr thought as Khilai came to a stop at last. She tilted her head back, the twinned spines of her headcrest fluttering slightly in the arctic breeze, as she stared up and up and up, her eyes finally reaching the bottom edge of the city's lowest arch. Beside her, Varakarr was straining backward to see as well. The city's shadow fell across them, engulfing them in darkness and cold, and both of them shivered again.

"How will we ever get up there?" Varakarr whispered, staring at the high gate looming so far above their heads. It might as well have rested within a cloud.

"How do you think?" she answered, raising her staff high. Varakarr quickly remembered himself and raised his own arms. Then both of them opened their mouths and began to sing.

The Mugic gathered around them, its melody weaving itself through the air and filling the space with Power. With that Power came light, streamers of brilliance that dispelled the shadows and then danced around the two Mipedians, forming a loose cocoon with them at the center. The cocoon began to rise, and it carried Khilai and Varakarr with it, lifting them into the air. As the ground fell away, the sun warmed them, and Varakarr almost sighed to feel blessed heat course through him once more. But he knew better than to falter in his song. The Mugic was powered by the melody, and if either of them stopped their singing, the cocoon might unravel, letting them crash back down to the snow and ice now far, far below. So they continued to sing, and the Mugic continued to ascend.

Their cocoon carried them up to the city's floating island, and Varakarr gaped at the land around the Citadel. It wasn't solid! Instead he saw several much smaller islands, all floating in the air near one another. Bridges and ropes and pulleys connected several of them. It was an amazing sight.

"We call that the Storms," Khilai explained as they floated across the array of tiny islands. "The Citadel Grounds are divided into four sections, and each displays one of the four Elements. The Storms reveal the Power of the Air."

Varakarr nodded. He had been taught about Kaizeph and the Citadel Grounds around it, of course. But seeing the Citadel and its island in person was still very different!

At last they brushed up against the bottom of the Storm Gate. The cocoon of magical light rebounded slightly, then floated forward again. This time it passed over the lip and wafted several yards into the city proper. Khilai lowered her staff and the Mugic set them down upon the wide, smooth polished flagstones of the Inner Yard as gently as a mother laying her child to rest. Then she closed her mouth, and as the last notes of the Mugic faded away so did the cocoon, its strands unraveling and drifting apart as tiny shimmers of light that finally were nothing more than sunlight against the air.

"We have arrived," she told Varakarr.

"And about time," a deep, rough voice growled nearby. Varakarr started, and only Khilai's hand on his arm kept him from jumping backward—which could have been disastrous, since they were still so close to the city's edge. He was sure his mentor could feel him trembling as a large, blocky shadow detached itself from a nearby wall and lumbered toward them.

"Time is hardly something we lack," Khilai told the approaching figure, a hint of reproach in her voice.

The powerful UnderWorlder stepped close enough that the shadows slid off him, and Varakarr stifled another gasp. Tall and broad-shouldered, with thick arms and a deep chest, he looked more like a Warrior than a Muge.

His large, taloned hands, massive horns, long fangs, and thick leathery wings only reinforced that impression. Those wings beat lazily behind him now, emphasizing his impatience. Varakarr couldn't help thinking that the hulking figure had them at a clear disadvantage, with those wings—of those in attendance he must be the only one who did not require Mugic to reach the city's gates.

"Gyrantin, High Muge of the UnderWorld," Khilai declared formally, raising her staff in front of her and letting the crystal at its peak burst into light. The light made her UnderWorld counterpart stumble to a halt, both hands raised to protect narrowed eyes, and she bit back a quick smile. "May I present my apprentice Varakarr of the Mipedians."

Faced with a formal greeting, Gyrantin growled but had no choice but to respond in kind. "Greetings, Varakarr of the Mipedians," he rumbled. "May the Mugic shine upon you and its light fill you with joy."

"And may its melody dance within you, granting you peace and prosperity," Varakarr answered, bowing deeply. He kept his posture erect, his bow perfect, and knew that he must present the very picture of a Mipedian Muge in his embroidered robes, with the light shining from each and every golden scale on his arms, hands, and head. The look of pride he saw in Khilai's eyes, and the brusque nod he got in return from Gyrantin, confirmed it. He was a Muge of Mipedim, and the High Mugess's personal apprentice. He would not allow the others to see him scared, even if he was quietly terrified.

"Come on," Gyrantin grunted finally. "The others are waiting." He leaped into the air and spread his wings, soaring up to the golden dome that hung suspended between the city's four towers. Varakarr glanced over at Khilai. She lowered her staff, letting its light fade, and nodded.

"Yes, enough theatrics," she agreed with just the hint of a laugh behind her words. "Come. It is time for the Meeting of the High Muges."

Khilai and Varakarr floated through the wide, arched window and landed gently in the golden Chamber of Emperors. The wide, circular floor was made of black stones fitted into a quartered radial pattern, each segment polished to a high sheen. The domed ceiling gleamed as well, and the two surfaces reflected the night sky that showed through the four wide windows so that it seemed they were walking among the stars. "Focus on the table," Khilai whispered as she felt her apprentice teeter beside her, and he nodded and breathed deeply, staring at the large, round table that stood off to one side of the enormous room. She remembered only too well the disorientation the chamber's mirroring effect could cause.

As they walked toward the crystalline table, Varakarr tried not to stare at the four massive thrones set in the center of the room. The Thrones of the four Elemental Emperors! Each throne belonged to one of them, and faced one of the chamber's four doors. Those doors each led to one of the towers—and to the Vortices! He gulped. The Power that lurked behind those four carved portals was staggering to consider. He forced his thoughts and his attention back to the meeting at hand, and had to hide a smile. Compared to thoughts of the Emperors, the Meeting of the High Muges was almost commonplace!

Almost.

Gyrantin had already flown to his seat on the table's far side and now sank down into it, the heavy stone frame groaning and creaking beneath his prodigious weight. Litik of the Danians sat beside him, his large faceted eyes partially hooded from impatience or disdain, or both, his two sets of forearms folded across his narrow, chitin-armored chest.

The individual in the third seat, however, gave them a warmer welcome, as Khilai had known she would.

"Ah, there you are!" Sonara rose from her seat with typical feline grace and came around the table to greet them, her long, soft tail waving slowly behind her. "And who have we here?" Sonara's slanted, almond-shaped eyes were wide with curiosity, and her striped, silvery fur ruffled with the breeze as she stalked closer, the blue of her flowing gown and cloak billowing out behind her. Beneath her cloak's hood Khilai could see her triangular, tufted ears swiveling forward to catch every word.

"Sonara, it is good to see you," Khilai answered, embracing her friend quickly. Of all the other Muges, past and present, Sonara was the one she felt closest to. "This is my apprentice, Varakarr. Varakarr, this is Sonara, High Mugess of the OverWorld."

"May the Mugic shine—" Varakarr began, but his words were cut off as Sonara threw her arms around him and gave him a quick, fierce hug.

"Oh, no need for ceremony with me," she assured him, her voice a velvety purr. "Any friend of Khilai's is a friend of mine. Now come, you two. Gyrantin's fit to burst and Litik might chew his own limbs off from impatience!" Khilai laughed at the image even as she let her friend drag them to the Mipedian chair. Smaller seats sat against the chamber's curving wall, reminders of a time when others joined them at their meetings, and Varakarr quickly fetched one and set it beside Khilai's, waiting until she was seated to sit himself. He was the only apprentice here, as Khilai had warned might be the case, and Khilai knew he felt more than a little out of place, and more than a little awed.

"Khilai," Litik stated from the opposite quarter of the round table, his voice dry.

She nodded in his direction, not quite meeting his faceted gaze. "Litik." Khilai knew from the rasping sound that followed that the Danian High Muge was rubbing his four arms together across his abdomen and his four legs together beneath the table, a sign that he was annoyed. Well, let him be. She and the Danian had never gotten along, though they fared better than many of their two races—the Mipedian and Danian Tribes disliked each other intensely, and fought wherever they met. Khilai suspected that old enmity had something to do with the two Tribes competing over the same food sources, and also the fact that they were so different, insect versus lizard, but disturbingly similar in some of their hierarchies and their rigid class structures. At least she and Litik could restrain themselves and be polite and cooperate, if coldly.

"And who is the youngling beside you?" Litik inquired cuttingly, his tone clearly indicating that he considered not being introduced to be a grave insult.

"Her apprentice, Varakarr," Gyrantin interrupted,

his wings beating against the back of his chair. "Can we get on with this?" He had his arms wrapped around his broad chest, and rubbed them. "I'm freezing to death!" As an UnderWorlder, he was accustomed to the lava flows and steam vents below the surface. The biting cold here was even more painful for him than it was for Khilai and Varakarr.

"I'm sure you'll survive a few more minutes," Sonara teased him, laughing outright when he growled back at her. The UnderWorlders and OverWorlders didn't get along, either—they were the most combative of the four Tribes, and often competed for territory, particularly along their shared borders at places like caverns and canyons and waterways—though at least in Sonara and Gyrantin's case, that was more about irritating each other than about any outright conflict. But of course Sonara was the most comfortable here, with her warm fur.

"Nonetheless, I call this meeting of the Council of High Muges to order," Litik declared formally. He raised his right upper forearm and sang the first word of a song of greeting, light pouring from his hand and flowing across the table. The traceries imbedded within its crystal facets glowed, reflecting and amplifying that light and the Power that went with it. Gyrantin, Sonara, and Khilai each raised their hands in turn and added to the song, the

Mugic growing between them, racing across the table and through it in an increasingly complex web, bonding them together. Varakarr kept silent, though the magic washed across him as he sat beside Khilai. He was here only to observe and learn, not to participate.

With the ritual completed, the meeting began. This time it was Litik's turn to lead, as it had been Khilai's the last and Sonara's before that and Gyrantin's before that. That way none of them ever felt slighted and all four remained equal.

"What news from the UnderWorld Tribe?" Litik asked Gyrantin, and Khilai resisted the urge to roll her eyes. Of course Litik would offer his UnderWorld ally the first chance to speak!

"No news," Gyrantin replied, wings aflutter. "All is quiet within the UnderWorld. Our people are safe and prosperous, our homes secure."

Litik nodded. "What news from the OverWorld Tribe?" he asked next.

Sonara's long tail curled behind her, swaying slightly as she spoke. "No news. Our people are happy and healthy. Our homes are safe. We live and laugh and play beneath the sun." She smiled, showing delicate fangs, and Khilai smothered a laugh. Sonara could always be counted upon to remind Litik and Gyrantin that their Tribes lived below the surface, while hers and Khilai's dwelled up here above ground.

Litik's large, crystal-like eyes blinked, registering the subtle insult, but he showed no other sign of having noticed. Instead he swiveled around to face Khilai. "What news from the Mipedian Tribe?"

Khilai had already worked out her answer, of course. "No news," she responded. "Our people are content and comfortable. Our homes are filled with light and music and warmth. The cool desert breeze caresses our scales and we shiver with delight." To her right, Sonora laughed in sheer appreciation even as Gyrantin growled.

Litik did not react, of course. She had rarely managed to get a rise out of him. But she did enjoy trying! "No news from the Danian Tribe," he reported, the words hissing out between his mandibles. "Our Hive is strong, our queen is healthy, and our people thrive below the Earth."

Everyone nodded.

"Is there anything else which must be brought to the High Muges' attention?" Litik asked officiously.

Khilai shook her head, as did the others.

"Very well. This meeting of the Council of High Muges is hereby adjourned," the Danian declared. "May the Mugic flow to us all, and may it bond us together as one just as this world is one."

Litik began the ritual of ending, and the others joined in. The Mugic that sparkled through the crystal table and lit the chamber strobed into brilliance and then flashed away, leaving only the starlight to fall through the windows and echo from the floor and ceiling. The meeting was over.

"Finally," Gyrantin grumbled as he pulled himself from his chair. He nodded at the others and then dove through the nearest window, straight past the tower there and down toward the ground below. Halfway down his wings spread open with a thunderous snap, catching the cold air and pulling him out of his dive and into a soaring flight. Within seconds he was only a dark shape on the horizon.

"Take care, my dear," Sonara said, embracing Khilai again before turning to make her way out of the chamber. "And it was a pleasure, young Varakarr. I'm sure we'll see each other at the next meeting," she called back over her shoulder. Litik had slipped away without a word, his sharp feet clattering on the stones, and Khilai and Varakarr found themselves alone in the Chamber of the Emperors.

After a second, Varakarr looked around. He seemed confused, even a little shocked. "That's it?" he asked finally.

"That's it," Khilai agreed, stepping away from the table and beckoning for him to do the same. "The meeting is over." She smiled at him. "Shall we go straight home—or would you like to see the Four Vortices first?"

Varakarr stood so quickly, he almost fell over backward, his eyes shining, and Khilai's smile turned into a broad grin. Oh, to be so young and eager again!

Chapter Two

"I don't understand," Varakarr admitted as he followed his mentor back across the chamber toward the window they had used as their entrance. He tried not to glance down, and gulped as he failed. From here he could clearly see the small clumps of land that made up the Storms—and between them to the gleaming lake far, far below. If he were to fall, there would be nothing to stop him from crashing into the lake and its ice-cold waters.

Still, he had questions and would not let his fear of falling distract him. "We came all this way," he continued, "just so we could sit and say 'no news'? And those other three did the same?"

"That is correct," Khilai responded. She passed by the window without a seeming care, but of course she had been here many times before. And she was the High Mugess—no doubt if she did stumble she could use her Mugic to save herself. Varakarr wasn't sure he could react quickly enough to say the same.

"But why bother to come at all, then?" was his next question. "It's a long, difficult journey for everyone involved. Why go all this way just to report that there is nothing to report?"

In front of him, he heard her sigh. Not a disappointed sound—he'd heard that one often enough during his studies, especially early on!—but one of fatigue and perhaps sorrow. "It is tradition," she explained softly, her words floating back to him as they continued to descend. "Every moon, the High Muges of each Tribe gather here, in the Citadel of the Elements, to discuss events that are affecting them and could affect Perim as a whole. Then they talk about ways to solve any problems, minimize conflict, and improve situations for everyone."

"But nothing happened!"

"No, and that is good," she replied. "There is nothing going on right now, or at least nothing important enough to bring to the others' attention. It is not always that serene." He saw a small shudder pass through her, rippling her crest. "You may be too young to remember the Wasting Sickness, but I know you have heard of it." Varakarr nodded. He had lost an aunt and two older cousins to the horrible disease, though he had been but an infant at the time, barely out of his sac. "The disease began among our people, and we could not contain it. None of us could find a way to fight it. I was only an apprentice myself then, but I came here with my master, High Muge Maranac. He told the other High Muges the situation, and they came to our aid." She shook her head. "It took the Muges of all four Tribes to stop the sickness, but they banished the disease forever. Our people were saved, and so were theirs, for if we had not eradicated it, the illness would have spread to the other Tribes as well. That is why the Council meets each moon."

"Even when there is nothing to report?" Varakarr asked.

"Even then. This way, if there is a problem, the rest learn about it within a matter of weeks at most. And if a High Muge fails to attend a Council meeting, the others know that something must be very wrong indeed." She glanced back at him and smiled. "That is why I brought you today, just as my master brought me so many turnings ago. Someday it will be your turn to attend these meetings, and the transition must go smoothly."

Fear gripped Varakarr's heart, and it had nothing to do with the lessening height around him. "That won't be for many turnings yet!" he stammered.

"No, it won't," Khilai agreed calmly. "But it is best to be prepared."

They continued their walk in silence, and Varakarr breathed a sigh of relief when they passed the window and reached the heavy golden door set beside it. He could not imagine entering this chamber each and every moon, but clearly it was a task he would have to resign himself to performing.

"Now," Khilai announced brightly, twirling her ornate staff in front of her, "let us go see the Four Vortices!"

Varakarr felt his pulse race again, this time with excitement. The Four Vortices! He had heard many tales of them, of course. Every Muge had, from their earliest training, and there were legends and stories besides. But to actually see them himself! It was an honor few attained, and Varakarr knew it showed his mentor's trust in him and his abilities that she would bring him to those sacred spots.

Khilai pulled the door open and it moved silently despite its size. Beyond was a small gap, and past that a wide arch that led into the Tower of the Air. Varakarr marveled again at the architecture all around him. Mipedian cities were short, squat things, with no buildings above two stories tall—the heat grew too unbearable at greater heights, and the desert winds too fierce. Most of their dwellings were domed to minimize impact from sun and wind, and made of baked clay and fired sand, then painted white and decorated in bright colors. Kaizeph was completely different. Its stonework was all gray and black and white, smooth and glossy but with flecks and streaks deep within. There was no paint, no decorations beyond the flowers and other shapes carved into doorframes and around pillars and jutting out from high corners. And everything towered here—the walls, the columns, the stairs all soared high above his head, many heights above, then ended with peaks and small plateaus and even decorative spheres. Wind whistled down every corridor, and cold seeped around every bend. Varakarr shivered. It was a stunning city, but he could not imagine living here.

"Who built this place?" he asked quietly, his words still echoing against the hard stone that surrounded them. "It was no Mipedian, I'm sure!"

"No one knows," Khilai admitted. "Kaizeph was discovered by Oronir, a High Muge of the OverWorlders, and one of the greatest Muges in the history of Perim." She paused and turned to face Varakarr, leaning on her staff. "It was he who first discovered the Vortices and brought them to the other Muges' attention. They say he crafted the crystal table as well, somehow imbuing it with Power so that its very structure amplified the Energy from the Vortices surrounding it. Back then, the Tribes were smaller and mingled more. They needed to in order to survive. There were even fewer Muges, and all worked together to protect Perim and its many people." She smiled, her eyes distant. "In fact, Oronir was not just the High Muge of the OverWorlders—he was *the* High Muge, and his word held sway over us all."

Varakarr shook his head. "Wait, there was only a single High Muge? And he was an OverWorlder?"

"Oronir was," Khilai agreed. "But before him came Drilinac, who was Danian. And before her was Cydec, one of our own people. And so on and so forth. A single High Muge directed the Muges at any given time, but he or she was the most powerful, most capable Muge alive, regardless of Tribe."

"So what happened to change that?" Varakarr asked.

She sighed and turned, resuming their trek toward the distant corner. "The Tribes grew apart. The old Muges conquered many of the world's dangers, as did the united Warriors of the four Tribes. Each Tribe settled in an area it found most comfortable, and that meant putting more distance between them and their neighbors. We are not happy in the jungles and forests and plains of the OverWorlders, who dislike the caves of the Danians, who are not happy in the lava beds of the UnderWorlders, and so forth. At first the Muges lived apart, tending to all the Tribes equally, but the distances became too great. Muges began staying with their Tribes instead, protecting them first and foremost." Her crest straightened and then fell again as her brow furrowed. "One of the Tribes—no one now knows which, or at least no one will admit to it—protested the appointment of the next High Muge, saying he or she was not from their Tribe and so knew nothing about their problems. They appointed a High Muge of their own instead. And so each Tribe selected its own High Muge. But those first four agreed at least to meet each moon, here in Kaizeph, the city Oronir had discovered and designated as a home and refuge and workplace for all Muges of every Tribe. By meeting here around his table, we try to remember that we were once a single unit, working together for the greater good."

Varakarr couldn't stop the dry chuckle that escaped him. "Clearly the memory grows dim."

"It does, but at least some semblance remains," Khilai reminded him, though the reprimand was mild. "As the Wasting Sickness proved, we can still work together when necessary, and that is what is important."

Khilai leaped across the gap between the chamber's door and the tower's arch, then beckoned for Varakarr to follow. He groaned in dismay, but his growing excitement overwhelmed his fear. The wall was decorated with stylized images, but all of them were representations of the same thing: the Air.

"Is this the Air Vortex?" he asked as he jumped across.

"It is," Khilai answered. "I thought you might like to see that one first, since it is our primary focus." Varakarr nodded. Mipedians worked heavily with Air Mugic. Danians concentrated on Earth, and the UnderWorlders were all about Fire Mugic, while the OverWorlders tended toward Water. He was curious to see all four Vortices, of course, but if they only had time for one, the Air Vortex was the one he would have chosen.

Khilai reached past him and shut the door again, hiding the Chamber of the Emperors from view. Then she led Varakarr up a short flight of steps to the open platform at the tower's peak. The floor here sloped gently down toward the center, where a recessed pool awaited. Within that circular pool swirled and floated pure Mugic, so intense Varakarr could feel his scales glowing from contact with the charged Air, and his crest bristled and stood at full attention. The melody hung in the air all about them, its rich but subtle song throbbing through him, setting his blood afire and making his senses reel. Khilai put a hand on his arm to steady him.

"Yes, it is intense," she assured him. "Especially the

first time." Her crest was raised as well, he saw, and her eyes glowed with light, as did the tip of her staff. Power radiated around her, the Mugic drawn to her, and Varakarr could see, as he could whenever she worked Mugic, why Khilai was their High Mugess. Her presence was magnetic, and he could barely tear his eyes away. Only the lure of the Air Vortex proved greater.

The Air Vortex. The source of all Air Mugic, or at least a wellspring of that Energy and Power—no one was quite sure if the Vortices were the origin or simply a gathering point. But what was certain was that this was the single greatest focal point for Air Mugic in all Perim, and that somehow Muges all over the world drew from it when they worked Air Mugic. It acted as a giant lens, helping them focus their Power and refine their spells, even from a distance. Its very existence granted them greater Mugical prowess. And now he stood here, staring into it! He could almost reach out and touch it!

"I wouldn't," Khilai warned, her staff crossing in front of his chest as he took an unconscious step forward. "Legends speak of Muges who touched the Vortices. They were absorbed into it, body and soul, and were never seen again." That snapped Varakarr out of his reverie, and he turned to gape at her. "Of course," she admitted with a small smile, "those are only legends. But best not to risk it, hmm? It took me some time to find an apprentice I liked. I'd rather not have to go through all that again."

He laughed with her then and gazed one last time upon the Air Vortex before turning away, back toward the stairs. "I'd hate to put you through so much work a second time," he agreed easily. "That would be horribly ungrateful of me."

"It would, wouldn't it?" Khilai said, her smile wider, as she joined him at the stairs again and they began their descent. The stairs continued on past the room that led to the Chamber of the Emperors, and Varakarr knew without asking that they would be following those steps all the way down to the Inner Yard below. "Now, would you like to see the other three Vortices as well?"

"Do we have time for that?" he asked. "It is a long journey home."

Now her smile was a full grin. "Oh, we won't be going back the long way," she assured him. "I can sing us home instead."

Varakarr turned, for he had started down the steps first, and stared up at his mentor. "You could have sung us here?" She nodded. "Then why did we endure that long trek instead?"

"I thought it best for you to experience the journey at least once," she explained calmly. "That way you could appreciate Kaizeph's location fully." She was still grinning. "And besides, a little exercise is good for you." The tip of her staff poked him in the stomach. "I'd hate for you to outgrow your robes."

"Hmph!" Varakarr turned and continued downward, shaking his head. Just because he was a little stockier than some didn't mean he was fat! But he had to admit, the trip here had been worth it for that first glimpse of the city floating above the valley. "Well, since we have time, yes, I would like to see the other Vortices. Please."

"Then we shall," she told him. "They are all worth viewing, and it is not often that we have Kaizeph all to ourselves. Normally we all leave together."

"Why?"

She laughed. "None of us trusts the others to stay behind—we're all afraid they'll find some way to use the Vortices to become more powerful than the rest of us."

"Is that really a possibility?" Varakarr asked her.

"I don't know," Khilai admitted. "But it's every Tribe's fear, that one of the others will become more powerful. Right now, and for as long as any of us can remember, the Tribes have been evenly balanced. None of us could overpower any of the others, and so we are at a constant stalemate. We skirmish along shared borders, seeking an advantage, but it is never enough to convince us that we could actually conquer and so we leave it at that." She sighed. "It is an uneasy peace, but a peace nonetheless."

"That seems a terrible way to live," Varakarr commented as they reached the Inner Yard again and began walking toward one of the other towers—they stood at the Inner Yard's four corners, with the Chamber of the Emperors suspended between them. "Isn't there some way to bring the Tribes together again?"

"We are each too wary of the others," Khilai answered. "None of us are willing to give any more than is necessary, and we hoard our Power and knowledge greedily, hoping that someday it will be enough."

"We should give it away instead," he argued. "If we contribute more, perhaps the others will as well. Then we can work past the mistrust and learn to cooperate more fully, as they did in ages past."

"You are young still," she told him, "and full of the optimism of youth. Most people would only see our generosity as weakness, and would seize it for their own advantage."

"But without trusting them, how can we be sure?" Varakarr insisted. "If no one ever takes that first step, nothing will ever change!"

"Perhaps not," Khilai agreed. "But at least it will not get any worse."

Varakarr did not argue further, but privately he thought his mentor was wrong. She was as set in her ways as the rest. It would take someone willing to take risks to break the old habits and traditions. Someone like him.

Chapter Three

Zartac glanced up, his ears pivoting as he strained to listen. All around him, his warriors saw the motion and fell silent, though many of them struggled to hear as well. It was difficult to pick out sounds with the Cordac Falls right beside them, but Zartac was sure he had heard something besides the rushing water. Where—? There!

"To arms!" he bellowed, snatching his great sword from his back and raising it high so its blade shone in the sunlight. "Prepare for battle!"

His squad was well trained, and jugs and canteens were tossed aside as weapons were unsheathed. In seconds, they stood in ragged formation, facing away from the water, prepared for whatever might emerge from the plains around them.

Now Zartac could hear the offending sound clearly. It was the march of feet, though perhaps "march" was too kind a description—he heard many feet, yes, but scrabbling and scraping in a chaotic mass, no order or regulation to it. Which meant it was neither one of his fellow patrols nor the Mipedians, whose scaled feet made a soft scrape against rock, nor the Danians, who moved in perfect formation. And that only left one Tribe—UnderWorlders!

Sure enough, as the sounds grew louder he was able to pinpoint their source, a large cavern in the rocks nearby. After a moment, Zartac could make out a flickering light there as well, and then shapes began to emerge against that light, their shadows stretching before them and emerging onto the rough ground around the Cordac Falls Plungepool long before the Creatures themselves. Though distorted by the dim light and by the rocky terrain, the shadows still revealed wings and tails and long, pointed heads and vicious claws.

Definitely UnderWorlders.

Finally the intruders themselves stepped forth. Zartac bristled, his mane standing on edge around his majestic head, his tail flicking with anger and eagerness combined. Let them come closer! Let them try!

They did come closer, close enough that he could make out individuals among the throng. They were an ugly lot! All scales and scabs and warts, talons and fangs and barbs and horns, glowing eyes, hooked beaks, and craggy features. Formidable, though, as he knew from personal experience. Only a few of them wore armor, but most carried weapons of some sort, axes and hammers and swords and spears and chains, and those without had elongated claws that looked more than sufficient on their own.

One of the UnderWorlders moved in front of the rest, and Zartac snarled, his lips pulling back from his own sharp teeth as he recognized the tall, gaunt figure with the jutting chin and bladelike nose and spiked ridges up and down his arms and legs and head and back. He might have guessed.

"What do you want here, Raritage?" he demanded, striding in front of his own warriors.

"Zartac!" the UnderWorld commander hissed, coming to a halt only a dozen paces from him. "What right have you to block our path? Stand aside!"

"Never!" Zartac answered. "The Cordac Falls belong to the OverWorld!"

"Don't be ridiculous," Raritage argued, his voice going soft and sibilant. "The Falls do not belong to anyone. All the Tribes may gain water freely here. You know this. Why do you seek conflict when there is no cause?"

Zartac knew that technically his rival was correct. The Cordac Falls were neutral territory, or at least universal property. The lands by the Glacier Plains were too cold for any of the Tribes to settle, but the water was ice-cold and pure, and the Cordac Falls were where that water gathered and plunged down below the surface. It collected in the wide Plungepool at its base, and all the Tribes gathered water there to bring back to their villages and cities. He had no particular authority here. But that didn't mean he had to admit to it.

"We were here first," he insisted. "Wait your turn!"

"There is plenty of room for everyone," Raritage pointed out, gesturing along the Falls. He was right, too. The Plungepool spread out from the Falls and ran from one side of the large cavern to the other, its length easily that of a hundred men side by side. Zartac and his men could collect water near one end, Raritage and his troops near the other, and they would still have a stone's throw between them.

But the UnderWorlders' arrival had left Zartac irritable, and he gave his temper free rein. "We were here first," he stated again. "Back away!" He had lowered his sword once his soldiers had gathered, but now he raised its blade before him again. "Or else."

Now Raritage hissed, his narrow, forked tongue flickering between his teeth, his eyes turning deep red, their glow lending a bloody hue to his face and features.

"You threaten us, OverWorld cur?" he spat. "How dare you? Stand aside, or face the consequences!"

"Ha!" Zartac brandished his sword higher. "Try your worst, you foul lava-eater!"

The insult woke a sharp, jagged cry from the UnderWorld leader and he raced forward, hands out and claws extended. Zartac leaped to meet him, both hands gripping his sword's handle firmly, his powerful arms bringing the weapon back to strike.

He never got a chance to connect. "Steam Rage!" he heard his rival declare, and then a torrent of boiling Air and Water shot toward him. Zartac twisted in midair so the blow took him in the back rather than the face, but still the impact propelled him back several lengths before knocking him off his feet.

"Ah, you wish to fight without honor!" he snarled as he pushed himself off the frozen ground. "So be it!" The last words came out as a roar so loud they buffeted the very air away, rippling out and making the frigid pool itself dance in reply. The sound wave caught Raritage full-force and slammed him back into his followers, knocking several of them to the ground.

"Don't just stand there gaping!" the UnderWorld commander shouted at his Warriors as he shoved them away and hauled himself back to his feet. "Attack!

Get the OverWorlders!"

"To battle!" Zartac replied, urging his own forces on.

The two patrols reached each other a second later. Weapons swung, as did fists, feet, heads, and tails. But weapons were not the only Attacks in play. Both sides were wielding Power as well; Flash Kicks and Inferno Gusts collided with bursts of light and Fire, while Frost Blights and Ember Swarms battled cold versus heat to see which would conquer. Warriors fell on both sides, but equal numbers. They were too well matched—neither force could gain an advantage.

Zartac had closed the distance with Raritage finally, but the UnderWorld commander had produced a short whip with several barbed strands, and the two traded blows and parries. Zartac could not get past Raritage's guard, while Raritage's whip did strike him several times but not hard enough to penetrate his thick fur.

At last the two paused, gasping for breath. They both had bruises and scrapes to show for their battle, but little more. The same was true for their Warriors.

"One of these days, Raritage," Zartac puffed, "I will crush you like the snake you are!"

"Not before I skin you and hang your fur coat upon my wall!" Raritage replied, though he was equally winded. The two glared at each other, before each signaled for a retreat. Both forces backed away warily, weapons still drawn though their tips scraped the rocky ground. None of them had strength left to fight, but they refused to turn their back on their old foes, either.

Within minutes, Raritage and his Warriors had retreated back into their cavern and disappeared from sight. Only then did Zartac call out to his own soldiers. "Gather the water jugs and skins," he commanded. "And make haste! Let us be gone before those foul Creatures return!"

His Warriors hurried to obey, and Zartac grabbed a skin himself, draining it quickly before dipping it again into the icy water of the Plungepool. The cold, clear draught refreshed him, but still he knew they could not withstand a second skirmish. But even in the cold climates his blood boiled at the thought of the stalemate he had suffered. Oh, to crush his foe instead! *One of these days,* he vowed as his patrol gathered its supplies and made ready to move out. *One of these days!*

Most of Glacier Plains' runoff flowed directly into the Cordac Falls and then collected within the Plungepool, but a few rivulets formed their own channels through the rocks below and drifted deeper into the UnderWorld. Some of these emerged again elsewhere in Perim, leading to rivers in warmer climates, and ultimately even to lakes or down to the Deep Ocean. One such stream flowed away from the Cordac Falls Plungepool off to one side, its passage narrow but deep, its waters seeming black even against the dark rocks all around.

And within that cold river, a pair of eyes gazed up at the OverWorlders as they marched off, leaving the Falls and beginning the trek back to their own Tribe's territory.

Herat'lat floated within the water, her long, narrow eyes still observing the OverWorlders' retreat, her pupil-less yellow gaze unwavering as she considered what she had just witnessed. So it was true that the OverWorlders and the UnderWorlders fought constantly! Yet it seemed neither had a clear advantage. The two commanders had obviously faced each other before, and though they had traded powerful blows, neither could claim the battle as a victory.

Herat'lat scratched idly at her cheek with one long tentacle as she organized her thoughts and impressions of the encounter she had just spied upon. They had suspected the dryworld Tribes valued the Cordac Falls, but this skirmish suggested it was a major water source for at least two of the Tribes. That was excellent information! Herat'lat's face split into a wide, lipless grin. The oligarch would be pleased with her.

She turned and began undulating her way back down the river, heading toward warmer waters and the Deep Ocean. Like all M'arrillians, she was at home in water, far more so than on land, but these particular stretches were a bit cool for her liking. She had come because she had been ordered to do so, and had accomplished her task. Now she could return and share the intelligence she had gathered with the leaders of her Tribe.

As she floated through the river's depths, her sinuous body wriggling in the current, Herat'lat considered what the drylanders would do if they knew she had seen them fighting. Would they have even known what to make of her? Most likely not! Few of them even knew of the M'arrillians, the fifth Tribe of Perim—and that was exactly how the oligarch wanted things. For now. They were too few to battle any of the dryland Tribes, and their fluid bodies and limber tentacles were ill suited for physical combat. Their strengths lay in their aquatic skills and in the Power of their minds. But that was not enough. They would never be able to best another Tribe, not the way matters stood now. That was why the oligarch kept them hidden in the ocean's depths, where the drylanders would never find them. And it was why she sent scouts like Herat'lat to keep tabs on the drylanders and bring back any information that might prove useful.

Herat'lat smiled again, her eyes and the tips of her feelers glowing to light her way through the dark waters. She was sure the conflict she'd witnessed would prove important to her leaders. And the sooner she reached M'arr, the sooner she could share her report with them. She picked up her pace, eager to reach the M'arrillian capital once more.

Chapter Four

"High Mugess! High Mugess!"

The shouts—and the pounding that accompanied them—startled Khilai, and she turned too quickly, almost toppling over. Fortunately her tail, still coiled on the floor behind her, compensated, and she was able to right herself and uncross her legs, stretching as she did so. She and Varakarr had been meditating as usual before discussing Mugical theory and practice. Normally no one disturbed them during this time, and she frowned. Something must be seriously wrong for the guards to come to her door with such urgency.

"Enter!" she called out, grabbing her staff and using it to push herself back to a standing position. Once she was stable enough she removed one hand from the staff and waved it at the door, which opened obligingly. The guard had been about to pound on it again, apparently, and almost fell into the room.

"Apologies, High Mugess!" he gasped, entering quickly but stopping a respectful distance away. "There has been a problem at one of the mines—your aid is desperately needed!"

"At one of the mines?" Varakarr had stood as well, and now stalked toward the guard, placing himself almost directly between him and Khilai. She cocked her head to the side as she pondered that move. Ever since their return from Kaizeph a few days ago, Varakarr had been behaving differently. It was hard to say exactly how, though. He seemed more forceful, more driven, and put more energy into his studies. At the same time, he was questioning her more, raising more difficult arguments during their discussions. But he also seemed a little . . . protective of her?

"Which mine?" he was asking the guard now. "And what sort of problem is it that the High Mugess would need to get involved?"

"It is the Stantin Mines," the guard answered, glancing from Varakarr to Khilai, clearly unsure toward whom he should be directing his answer. He settled finally on Khilai. "I don't know the details. One of your Muges was there and sent a message to fetch you at once."

Khilai nodded. "Firizon had mentioned she wished to observe the mining there," she reminded Varakarr.

"She was curious whether Mugic might aid the process." Now she was concerned. Firizon was a good Muge, smart and clearheaded and quick. If she had called for aid, something was terribly amiss.

"We must go at once," she decided. Varakarr knew what that meant. He stepped closer to her as she raised her staff, so that the light now emanating from its tip bathed them both. Then he joined his voice to hers as together they sang a Song of Translocation.

Khilai's study vanished around them, replaced by a gleaming rainbow ribbon of light that wove itself about faster and faster, until all they could see were traces of brilliant color everywhere. The ribbon moved with their song, dancing to its melody, and as the song ended it began to slow. Gaps appeared within its weave, and through them Khilai could see glimpses of rock and sand and a wide, dark opening. The Stantin Mines.

Khilai had not been here for some time, and she took a second to regain her bearings and look around. Much of the mines looked the same. The miners had found a natural cave in the rocks of the Stantin Hills, as this outcropping was called—it was one of the largest rockpiles in the desert, and so had attracted interest from the moment of its discovery. But exploring the cave had led to something even more exciting, for there were ores threaded through the cavern walls below. The Mipedian Kingdom was rich in sand and glass but poor in metal, and a fresh source of iron, steel, and copper was a true treasure.

Since that initial discovery, the cave mouth had been widened significantly, thick timbers used to brace it, and tracks cut deep into rock and sand where wheeled carts were used to haul ore back out for smelting. The entire area smelled of torch smoke and metal shavings, a sharp, acrid smell that tickled Khilai's nostrils and threatened to make her sneeze. Beside her, Varakarr succumbed to the temptation, honking loudly and then looking embarrassed.

"There's no shame in sneezing," she chided her apprentice gently. "It is a natural process." Still, his loud sneezes had amused her, which took a little of the edge off the tension, and for that she was grateful.

The relief did not last long, however. Something about the scene here was bothering her, and after a few seconds, Khilai realized what it was. The quiet. Where was everyone? It was still a few hours before sunset, when the area would become too cold to work comfortably and too dark to work safely. Normally the mines would be teeming with activity right now. Yet it was utterly silent.

No, not utterly, she corrected herself. She could hear

something, very faintly. It sounded like—hissing?

"I hear it, too," Varakarr confirmed when she glanced at him. "I think it's coming from within the mines."

Yes, that made sense. Khilai moved slowly toward the cave entrance, listening intently. There it was again! Varakarr was right—it was definitely coming from inside there, somewhere in the darkness.

"Be careful," he whispered as he fell in behind her. "Whatever it is, it must have been too much for Firizon."

Khilai nodded but didn't bother to reply otherwise. At least Varakarr had recognized that he would probably also be no match for whatever it was, and had not attempted to precede her. Right now she needed a clear view of whatever awaited them. With a thought, she relit the tip of her staff, and holding it before her like a torch she entered the cave.

A cart stood just within the mouth, filled to the brim with chunks of ore. So the miners had been working, and then had stopped. Something must have happened, but what? And where were they all? Had they run away? Or were they near that strange sound, and unable to call out or escape? Khilai felt her crest stiffen, each spine standing straight as her entire body tensed. She could already feel that something was down there. Something Mugical.

She crept on, slow but steady, unwilling to run into

anything unprepared. Her staff's light threw long shadows against the walls as she and Varakarr passed cart after cart. But still no sign of the miners. Or Firizon.

And the sound grew ever so slightly louder.

The way wound downward, a passage naturally formed from the surrounding rock but then widened with picks and chisels and hammers. Torches stood in iron sconces along the way, most of them still lit, but Khilai kept her staff aglow as well. She wasn't fond of the dark, and anything that had come from within the caves was likely to dislike the light as much or more. That could work to her advantage—and right now she suspected she might need whatever advantage she could find.

The sound was definitely louder now, and definitely hissing. Had the miners stumbled upon an UnderWorlder? But surely a single UnderWorlder would have posed no threat to the sturdy miners, or to Firizon, and she could hear only a single sound. Was it some sort of natural phenomenon instead? Perhaps a pickax had breached some new underground chamber, and the sound was that of gas escaping? But surely the miners would have fled and sealed off that area, and would have been waiting for her near the entrance. None of it made sense.

At last she rounded a bend, and stopped. There

before her lay the answer—but she didn't understand it.

She processed what she saw. The tunnel opened into a wider chamber, a natural cavern judging from the rough walls. The miners were all here, and she thought she caught a glimpse of robes as well, but wasn't sure. No one was moving.

No one except the snake.

Khilai had seen a cave snake once before, and recognized it, with its rock-colored scales and wide, clear eyes. The Creatures lived in the darkness of caves and tunnels, their coloring allowing them to blend into their surroundings, their overlarge eyes picking up the tiniest traces of light and letting them strike anything that stumbled past. Cave snakes also had an excellent sense of vibration, she recalled as she slowed to a stop, and could sense movement nearby, letting them attack even in complete darkness.

This was a very large snake, much bigger than the one she'd seen previously, but even so she was puzzled. Cave snakes had a nasty bite, and those attacked could grow ill if the wounds were not treated quickly, but normally one would be no threat to a grown Mipedian. An entire mining operation? They would have sent two or three miners in with torches and pickaxes to blind and disable the snake and then kill it, and that would have been that.

Yet clearly that was not the case here. Because all of the miners were here, as was the snake—and no one was attacking it. In fact, as Khilai watched, amazed, the snake glided up to one of the miners, reared back, and bit him on the leg.

The miner didn't cry out. Or flinch. In fact, he didn't move at all.

Were they all dead? But no, Khilai could still sense the Energy pulsing within each of them. They were alive, just immobile. How had this happened? And why wasn't the snake affected?

Unless it was somehow the cause of this strange paralysis.

Softly, Khilai sang a Song of Truesight, using the Mugic to enhance her senses and let her study the scene more closely. Varakarr was doing the same beside her, their voices harmonizing to strengthen the effect. When the song was done, Khilai opened her eyes again—she had shut them as she'd sung, so that the effect would not disorient her—and gasped. The entire chamber was filled with Power! She could see its strands everywhere, laced over each and every miner, and over Firizon as well. The Muge shone more brightly than the others as her own Mugic glowed within and around her, but she was just as trapped as the rest.

And the cave snake? It glowed as well, but those strands were emanating from it. It had somehow bedazzled the miners so that it could strike them at will!

Well, now that she knew what she was seeing, the problem was easily solved. Khilai raised her staff and sang a quick negation, canceling the Song of Stasis that the cave snake had somehow cast. As her words echoed through the chamber, the miners' bodies relaxed. They began to breathe normally again, and to blink, their eyes tearing from being open too long and from the light of her staff. And then they began to move, to whisper, to shout, and to cry out as they remembered the horror of their situation.

"This way!" Varakarr called out to them, and everyone turned to see him and Khilai standing near the entrance. "Quickly, but without panicking! You will all be fine!"

The nearest miners stumbled toward them, gasping out thanks, and Varakarr nodded and motioned them along. They obeyed, making room for the next few, and he continued to direct them, leaving Khilai free to watch the cave snake. Its hissing had grown louder as its prey had begun to escape, and she could see it weaving about angrily, its head bobbing as it searched for fresh victims. It would strike at the miners again. Unless she stopped it.

"Take care of them," Khilai told Varakarr as she brushed past him, and he nodded, already busy doing just that. Firizon hurried toward her, mumbling apologies and warnings, but Khilai waved her off as well. She already knew the danger, and could not afford any distractions.

The cave snake turned its head toward her as she approached, its eyes closed to mere slits from the light but her footsteps letting it locate her without vision. It hissed, its wide mouth gaping open to reveal its dripping fangs, and she felt its Power rear up and lash out. She was prepared, however, and raised her staff in front of her, a Song of Deflection already spilling from her. The Attack glanced off the magical shield, but even so its sheer force staggered her. How did a cave snake come by such Power?

The snake's tongue was flickering between its fangs now, and it hissed and spat at her, clearly angry that she had not succumbed to its initial Attack. It slithered closer, and Khilai advanced as well. It was dangerous to get within striking range of those fangs, she knew, but she would need to be close enough to deal with the Creature properly. And it definitely had to be dealt with, once and for all.

A second wave of Power battered at her, and again she warded it off. By the king's crest, it was strong! Now only a few feet separated them, and the snake reared up physically, mouth open wide, fangs glittering in her staff's light. It was going to bite!

But Khilai was ready. She had already started humming in the back of her throat, and now she opened her mouth and began to trill. Swirls of color arced out around her and spun toward the cave snake even as it launched itself forward, fangs first. Khilai raised her staff as a final defense and shuddered as the snake's fangs sank into the carved wood just shy of her hand. Then the Mugic wrapped around the cave snake, and it stiffened, its eyes dimming as the Trills of Diminution did their work. The Mugic blocked the Creature's own Power, reverting it to a normal if large snake, and Khilai wasted no time using that opportunity. She was not sure she could remove the snake from her staff, so she sang an Interlude of Consequence instead, willing the Mugic to alter the snake as she desired.

She watched as the snake's body wrapped the rest of the way around her staff, its head draping over the crystal at the top. Its body changed color, turning silvery, and its eyes became crystals. The change affixed itself even as she felt the snake's mind stir again and its Power begin to return. But it was too late. The snake was now frozen as a staff. It could no longer bite, and its ability to wield

Mugic was now controlled by whoever wielded the staff. Meaning her.

The danger had passed.

Or had it? She could still feel much of that same Power in the staff, though now it was constrained by its new form. And it was still far beyond anything she had encountered in any Creature, and more than most Muges, either. How had a mere cave snake come to possess such a mighty gift?

Curious, Khilai studied her new staff. She could see the center of the Power, both as a swirl of Energy and as a visible lump a third of the way down the snake's body. Using the Interlude of Consequence again, she drew the shape out of the snake, passing it through the Creature's altered and hardened flesh until she held a large, glowing rock in her other hand. Its song rang through her head as her flesh came into contact with it, and Khilai knew without a doubt that this was the source of the Power she had sensed. The cave snake must have swallowed it, and that had granted it the Power to sing a Song of Stasis.

But what was it?

Well, Khilai decided as she rose to her feet, the rock still clutched in one hand and her new staff in the other, she would have to find out.

Chapter Five

Back in her chambers, Khilai set the strange rock down on her worktable. Then she perched on a stool, folded her arms on the table, laid her head upon them, and stared at the glowing object. What was it?

She focused her senses, her mind, and her Mugic upon it. On the surface, it was a rock, plain and simple. Not the sort of rock the Stantin Mines were carved from, which meant it had come from some distance away or from well below the caverns and mines there. That would explain the cave snake. The miners had reported larger and more ferocious Creatures the deeper they dug into the Earth, in the same way those few Mipedians who braved rivers and lakes told of fish and crabs and other life that grew larger and fiercer the farther down they dove. The cave snake had been massive, its scales thicker and more like armor, its eyes wider and paler—it must have come from a great depth indeed. And if it had brought the rock with it in its journey toward the surface, well, there was no telling how deep the rock had been buried before!

But buried how? Or by whom? Khilai continued to study it. It was vaguely round but its shape was as rough as its dented, pitted surface. No one had carved this! And she was sure the rock itself was natural. The Power within it was a different matter, however. So how had a simple rock from somewhere deep underground gained such potent Energy?

The UnderWorld—Khilai wondered if they could be responsible. But she quickly dismissed the thought. She knew UnderWorld Mugic, and this carried no trace of that Tribe's involvement. Its song was entirely different and completely unique. Besides, the UnderWorld Muges were not given to experimentation much. They were far too focused on practical Mugic, particularly that of conquest and destruction.

Which led to the next question—what exactly was the rock's Power? It had granted the cave snake a Song of Stasis. Was that the extent of its abilities, or did it contain—or somehow facilitate—other songs as well? The snake still possessed Power, even now. She glanced at her staff and smiled. For all the good that would do it. Nor was this the first rock to contain Mugic. Her eyes slid to the crystals sitting upon a shelf along one wall. Each had been fashioned by one of her predecessors, and contained a powerful song within its facets. The crystals also bore traces of the Muges themselves, and on the rare occasions where Khilai had used one, she had felt the spirit of the Muge in question, aiding her and working through her. That was not the case with this rock, however. It had bore no spirit, and no specific song, just pure Power.

Khilai groaned and rubbed her crest with one hand. There was so much about it she didn't know! All she could say for certain right now was that it was a real rock, it was from deep underground, and it contained enough Power to grant a dumb beast potent Mugic. But she felt like she had only just scratched the surface of the rock's origins—and of its potential.

A knock on the door startled her, and she jumped. As she did, her hand swept across the worktable and brushed against the rock. The instant surge she felt made her stop cold. She glanced down at it again, then deliberately touched it with her right forefinger. Yes, there! The second she came in contact with the rock, its melody burst into her head. In fact, it threatened to overwhelm her, it was so loud and powerful. She felt herself being swept away in its music. But she resisted, and slowly managed to force the tune to the back of her mind. It continued to thrum through her, but now she could think again. She turned her thoughts back to the rock, and studied it through the point of physical connection.

The Power! It contained a veritable sun, bursting with Mugical Energy! It was the most glorious thing Khilai had ever felt, and once again she felt it trying to overpower her. She forced it back down, though it took some effort. She wasn't sure how much longer she could fend off its advances. They weren't Attacks, though—she didn't sense a consciousness in the rock at all. It was an object, albeit an immensely powerful one.

All of its might was directed along a single path, however. She could feel that. It had no elemental Mugic in it, no Fire or Earth or Air or Water. Nor was its Power physical in nature, or healing. No, it was all about the songs and melodies and the thoughts—all about the mind. The mind! That was it! Somehow the rock contained vast amounts of mental Power! That was why the cave snake had been able to paralyze everyone in the mines. It had attacked and frozen their minds!

Khilai pulled her finger from the rock, feeling the connection stretch and finally snap with an almost audible sound. She sighed at the sudden separation—she felt dim and quiet and drab and empty without its music rushing through her head. She would have to be very careful. It would be all too easy to become used to that song, to the point where she could not survive without it.

The knock came again, and only its return reminded her that she had not answered the first time. "Enter," she called out, gesturing the door open, and Varakarr stepped in.

"Ah, I thought you might be studying that thing," he said as he closed the door behind him and joined her by the worktable, dragging over another stool. "I can feel it from across the room! What is it?"

"I don't entirely know," Khilai confessed. She explained to her apprentice what she'd felt so far, and what type of Power the rock seemed to contain.

"That could be incredibly useful," Varakarr commented, staring openly at the stone.

"I agree, but we'll need to find some way to contain its song," Khilai said. She stroked her crest again, thinking. "Right now it's too powerful, too likely to overwhelm anyone who touches it. We have to make it safe."

"So we need to bind it."

She nodded. "Yes. But perhaps we can focus it at the same time." A plan was beginning to shape itself in her head.

Over the course of the next week, the two of them studied the rock exhaustively. They used their songs to examine it inside and out, studying every aspect. Each test, each perusal, matched what Khilai had already seen—and suggested that her plan should work perfectly.

Once they were satisfied, she and Varakarr got started. They shaped the rock, carving away its imperfections and blemishes and irregularities, smoothing its surface and perfecting its shape. It had been roughly spherical to start, and so they had decided to make it a proper sphere. Khilai reasoned that the round, never-ending shape would serve as both a lens and a prison for the rock's Energy, focusing it but also keeping it tightly bound within. The fact that they were using Mugic to do the shaping, rather than mundane tools, added a mystical coating to the stone, reinforcing the restrictive nature of its new shape but also making the Power within easier to access.

When the sphere was finished, they worked on the power itself. More songs were sung, these melodies layering themselves into the rock's own song and mingling there to create a new, richer, subtler harmony. Music and magic were one, and so as the song grew more controlled and more intricate, so too did the magic. The rock's Power was tightly focused now, and even more tightly restrained. It could no longer overpower its wielder, focusing all its considerable might on the wielder's designated targets instead. It had gone from being a strange object of nature to a true Mugical artifact—and a weapon.

Three weeks after the incident at the mines, Khilai called all of her Muges together. She met with them in one of the palace's inner courtyards. Though there were only twelve in all, her rooms were nowhere near large enough to comfortably hold such a number.

"Most of you heard about Firizon's encounter with the cave snake," she began, waving her new serpent-staff at them and getting several laughs and a few good-natured jokes at Firizon's expense. "None of you would have fared any better," Khilai reminded them archly, and the murmurs quieted. "The cave snake had swallowed a strange rock, something it must have found in a deep cavern somewhere. That rock granted it tremendous Power, so much that I was barely able to defeat it in mental battle." The murmurs were replaced by gasps and stares, and Khilai smiled. It was good to know her Muges still respected her Power.

"Afterward, Varakarr and I studied the rock," she continued. "We decided its Power was too wild, too unrestrained, too unfocused. It would be a danger to anyone who touched it. So we reshaped it, refining both the rock and the Power within. And the result—is this!" She raised her right arm, letting her robe's wide sleeve fall back to reveal both her hand and the large stone sphere cradled by it.

This time the gasps were of admiration. And for good reason. She and Varakarr had labored long and hard, and the result was a perfect sphere of polished rock, its surface a mixture of gray, black, and silver. The three were woven together in no discernible pattern and also no end, writhing and twisting around and through one another in an endless parade of shape and color. The silver sparkled in the late afternoon light, the black shone, and the gray produced tiny rainbow flecks of color. It was breathtaking.

"The rock's Power has been focused into this sphere," she explained. "It is entirely mental in nature, and will boost the psionic gifts of any who touch it. We believe that enhancement can even be shared with others." Actually, she and Varakarr had tested the theory, and were fairly certain they were right. She had been able to touch the sphere, tap its Energy, and then give that Energy freely to Varakarr. The boost was only temporary, but it was still intense. "Here, try it." She held out her hand and stepped closer to the nearest Muge, who turned out to be Firizon. She looked startled at being offered the sphere, but after a second, she took it.

"Amazing!" Firizon whispered the second her scales

touched its polished surface. “I can hear its song echoing through my head!” Firizon was a tall, broad Mipedian, her wide, flat snout seeming to curve back in a permanent smile that hid rows of small sharp teeth, her cheerful eyes set far apart on either side of that broad face, her skin bumpy and a deep green. Now her eyes glowed from within and her skin took on the appearance of green marble, glossy and smooth but iron-hard as she raised the sphere to eye level and stared at it, unblinking.

“Reach out to me with your mind,” Khilai urged. For a second Firizon hesitated, but then she turned and fixed Khilai with her gaze. Khilai felt the power coiling about the other Muge, and then it swept toward and over her like a wave, engulfing her completely. She struggled against it, but to no avail. All her defenses had been washed away in that first instant, and now she stood helpless and powerless before Firizon’s Mugic, and the other song that wove through it.

“That was incredible!” Firizon whispered, handing the sphere back reluctantly. “I crashed right through your defenses!”

“Yes, it magnifies the wielder’s mental gifts,” Khilai explained, accepting the sphere again and moving on to the next Muge, a spindly, long-limbed fellow named Ganott. “With a Muge, it adds to our existing Mugic, enhancing even the weakest song beyond even my ability to break." She passed the sphere to him, and let him test its power against her as well.

"This is fantastic!" he enthused as he gave it back and she moved to the Muge past him. "With this device we could easily crush anyone who tried to stand against us! We could bend all the other Muges to our will! The Mipedian Kingdom could reign supreme!"

"Perhaps," Khilai agreed. "But we have no idea what long-term effects it might have, either on its wielder or on those who face its Power. It could drive us mad, or them, or both. It could gradually harden them to psionic Power, until they became immune to its Attacks. We simply don't know yet." She sighed. "Besides, why would we want to rule Perim? Isn't our own kingdom enough? Let the other Tribes have their territories. We wouldn't want to live there, anyway! The desert is our home!"

"True," another Muge, Biginth, agreed. "But at least now, with this, we can withstand any Attack any of the other Tribes could throw at us. Even if we only use the sphere for defense, it is a formidable weapon."

"You've provided the ultimate protection for our people," Firizon added. "The Khilaian Sphere!"

"The Khilaian Sphere!" the others shouted after her, Varakarr among them. Khilai smiled and accepted their enthusiasm and their congratulations. At the same time, she knew deep down that she would avoid using the Sphere unless absolutely necessary. She still had a bad feeling that its power was too much for anyone, including her, to control.

Chapter Six

"What news from the Mipedian Tribe?"

Gyrantin glowered at Khilai even as he posed the question, his gleaming red eyes stabbing into her from beneath his heavy brow. Beside him, Litik was also intent upon her, his wide faceted eyes as unblinking as ever but somehow seeming more intent, perhaps because of the way his antennae and mandibles were twitching eagerly. Even Sonara was studying Khilai openly, her tail waving behind her, both ears swiveled forward, whiskers aquiver.

Khilai steepled her fingers on the faceted table in front of her. "No news," she told the other three High Muges. Beside her, she felt Varakarr shift slightly, covering his surprise, but she did her best to ignore him as she continued her report. "Our people are safe and healthy, our food plentiful, the sun warm and life-giving, the desert cool and nurturing."

For a second, no one responded. No one even blinked.

Then Gyrantin shifted his bulk, the chair beneath him groaning in protest. "Are you sure there is no news?" he rumbled. "Nothing of interest to the Council?"

"We are fine," Khilai insisted. "All is well within the Mipedian Kingdom."

"And is there aught that should be brought to the Council's attention?" Gyrantin persisted. He leaned forward, looming at her even across the wide table, his craggy features blocking out the starlight behind him. "Nothing new and unusual of a Mugical nature?"

Khilai refused to be intimidated. "If you have something to say, Gyrantin, I suggest you say it," she told the UnderWorld High Muge. "Subtlety was never your strong point."

"Fine." He scowled, his fangs tugging at the edges of his lips. "A few weeks ago, I felt something. Something strange. Something powerful. Something Mugical." He jabbed a thick, taloned finger at her. "Something that emanated from your Tribe's lands! Something has happened there, and you are keeping it from us!"

Litik nodded, his mandibles clacking together. "Yes, we felt it as well," he agreed, quick to side with his UnderWorld ally. "It was unfamiliar but strong, so very strong. We would very much like to know what that was."

Even Sonara chimed in. "We respect your privacy, of course," she told Khilai, giving the other two High Muges a quick glare, "and if this was merely a new song we would not even ask. But it felt . . . different. The Mugic did not match your people's melody. And that concerns us."

"I have fashioned a new staff," Khilai pointed out, gripping the serpent-headed staff she had laid across her lap and raising it so the snake's crystal eyes caught the light. "My students have taken to calling it the Serpentotem."

"A powerful tool, to be sure," Gyrantin agreed. "Yet that is not the strength I felt, though there is some similarity." Litik and Sonara nodded.

Khilai sighed. She had known, coming here, that the other High Muges might ask about the Sphere. It was too powerful to keep secret for long. But she had decided to hope for the best, and had cautioned Varakarr not to say anything, either.

Now she nodded slightly. "We found something," she admitted slowly. "An . . . object. It contains Power, but it is dangerous to those who touch it, and to those around them. We are studying it." She could feel Varakarr beside her, straining to speak, and gave him a quick, sharp look and a tiny shake of her head. His crest rose defiantly, but he stayed silent.

"Perhaps we could help unlock this object's secrets," Sonara all but purred at her. "We could work together, for the safety of all."

"Thank you, but that is unnecessary," Khilai assured her friend. "We have the situation under control."

"If this is some new source of Mugic, it concerns us all," Litik insisted. Gyrantin growled his agreement, and Sonara seemed ready to side with them as well, despite her obvious distaste at having to agree with the Danian and UnderWorld High Muges on anything. But before she could speak, Khilai stood, cutting them all off.

"No, it does not," she insisted sharply. "The object was found on Mipedian soil. It is the property of the Mipedian Kingdom." She forced herself to sit back down and lower her crest, which had been standing on end, and softened her tone to match. "I appreciate your interest, and your concern, but I assure you, you have nothing to worry about. And while I realize you are curious, the object is neither powerful enough nor dangerous enough to pose a threat to Perim in general, and so it is not something the Council needs to be concerned about. It is a Mipedian matter, and we will deal with it ourselves." She prayed that Varakarr would keep his mouth shut and let her lie stand. And for once he did, though she knew she would hear about it later, after the Council meeting.

For a second, she thought the others might argue further, but then Sonara nodded. "If you say this is a Mipedian matter, we believe you," she assured Khilai. "You are our friend and our colleague, and we trust you. Perhaps, in time, you will share with us what you have learned about the object, and about the Mugic it contains?"

Khilai nodded her thanks. "Of course," she agreed readily. "Once we have discovered all of its properties, we will be happy to share that information." That was a safe enough thing to promise—she doubted they would ever know everything about the Sphere!

The others seemed to sense her duplicity, and Litik clacked his mandibles again, his antennae waving wildly, while Gyrantin snorted and bared his fangs in a full grimace, the beginnings of a growl deep in his throat. But neither of them commented further, and after a second, Gyrantin settled back in his chair.

"No news from the UnderWorld," he rasped. "All is quiet within our realm. Our people are safe and prosperous, our homes secure." They were almost the same words he had spoken at the last Council meeting, but then Gyrantin didn't bother coming up with new and clever ways to say "all's well" each time. "Is there anything else which must be brought to the High Muges' attention?"

he asked, looking straight at Khilai. The others turned toward her again as well, all leaning in across the crystal table, clearly hoping she had changed her mind. But she shook her head and kept her mouth tightly shut.

"Fine," Gyrantin declared finally. "This meeting of the Council of High Muges is hereby adjourned." He closed his eyes and tilted his head back, his voice lifting as he set some of his habitual rage aside to begin the ritual of ending. "May the Mugic flow to us all, and may it bond us together as one just as this world is one."

The rest of them joined him in the ritual, and the Mugic flared above and around them, then faded. Khilai was out of her chair the instant the mystical light disappeared, and gestured for Varakarr to make haste as well.

"Leaving so soon?" Sonara asked, gliding up beside them. "I'd hoped we'd find time to sit and chat a bit before we left. It has been a while since we've caught up properly."

"I know, and I'm sorry," Khilai told her, and meant it. "But we need to get back home right away." She hated lying to her friend, especially when they both knew it was a lie, but consoled herself with the knowledge that Sonara was being false as well. They were friends, and it had been some time since they'd really talked, but right now the

OverWorld High Mugess was only interested in talking about one thing—the Sphere. She was hoping Khilai would reveal more about it and its Power if they talked, perhaps by accident or perhaps in confidence. And Khilai couldn't risk her being right.

"Of course," Sonara murmured. "Some other time, then." She leaned in and gave Khilai a quick hug, nodded to Varakarr, and then stalked off. By tradition no Mugic was used in the Chamber of the Emperors except the rituals of joining and ending, and so Khilai led Varakarr back into the Tower of the Air and down to the Inner Yard before singing the Song of Translocation to carry them home. Gyrantin had thrown himself out one of the chamber's windows again, of course, and Litik had simply vanished—whether he'd hurried into the Tower of the Earth or lurked in a shadow afterward or somehow cast a song there without anyone noticing, Khilai had no idea, nor did she care. Right now she just wanted to be well away from the other High Muges, before things grew even more awkward.

"We should have told them about the Sphere," Varakarr told her the second they were back in her chambers, the Mugic already dissipating around them. "We should have been honest about it, maybe even brought it to show them."

Khilai shook her head. "That would have been too dangerous," she insisted. She had considered bringing the Sphere with her, just so she knew where it was at all times, but had decided it would be safer here, under guard.

"Why did you lie to them?" her apprentice demanded. "Why didn't you tell them the truth about where we found it, what we did to shape it, and what it can do?"

"Because then they'd want to see it!" she shot back. "And then they'd want to touch it! And then they'd want to use it!"

"So what?" Varakarr was pacing around the room. "Why is that such a bad thing? They're the High Muges! Your peers! Isn't the Council supposed to work together?"

"Only when something puts all of Perim at risk," Khilai corrected, trying to douse her own rising temper. "This isn't something that concerns them."

"It could!" Varakarr insisted. "It's dangerous, and you know it! Any Muge armed with the Sphere could overpower any of us, probably all of us together!"

"Which is exactly why we can't tell them about it!" she yelled. "If any of them got their hands on it, they would be able to overpower us all! They'd crush our Tribe completely!"

"You don't know that," he claimed, but his voice had

dropped and he looked down at his hands. "They might genuinely wish to share the knowledge."

"They might," she agreed. "At least, Sonara might. But Gyrantin dreams of conquest, and Litik serves only the glory of the Danian Hive. Either of them would see the Sphere for what it could be, a weapon, and would want to use it as such. And Sonara might have good intentions, but how long could she resist the temptation? She dislikes Gyrantin as much as I hate Litik, and her people have been at war with the UnderWorlders for generations. With the Sphere, she could end that battle once and for all. How long before she did so? And after the UnderWorlders, why not the Danians? And then us?"

"She's your friend," Varakarr argued, but quietly.

"I know she is," Khilai answered. "But it's too much temptation for anyone, even her." *Maybe even me,* she thought privately. Thus far she'd resisted the urge to use the Sphere, and contented herself with studying it. But she couldn't be sure how long she could hold out, either. Especially with several of her Muges encouraging her daily to use it and advance their Tribe. She had yet to tell King Kehn-Sep anything other than that she had fashioned a Mugical artifact, and that she was still studying it. He was a good ruler, but she still worried that he might order her to use the Sphere against the other Tribes.

And if he did, how could she say no?

"You underestimate people," Varakarr was saying. "You don't give them a chance to prove themselves, which forces everything to stay exactly as it is."

"There's nothing wrong with the way things are," Khilai told him. "The world is at peace, the Tribes existing side by side. Anything that unbalances that would cause turmoil, conflict, and most likely war. Is that what you want?"

He shook his head. "Of course not. But we will never be one people united again if we keep ourselves apart." He turned toward the door. "That Sphere might be the thing to unite us."

Khilai watched him go. "Or," she whispered as the door shut behind him, "it might be the very thing to tear us all apart."

Chapter Seven

Many leagues away, and many more leagues below the surface, others had sensed the Sphere's presence as well. But they had not sent a representative to the Council of High Muges. Indeed, they had no Muges, though some among them did possess strong mystic Power. These were the Fluidmorphers, the Mugical elite among the M'arrillians. When the Sphere had been created, many of those same Fluidmorphers had gathered, in the M'arrillian city of M'arr on the floor of the Deep Ocean, to discuss the strange presence they had all felt.

"It is a powerful force," they had all agreed. "Somewhere on dryland. But what? And where?"

"I am less concerned about the where," one of them, an ambitious young Fluidmorpher named M'ahadil, argued, "and more about the whom. Who among the drylanders possesses such power, and what do they mean to do with it?"

The M'arrillians urged their scouts to bring them news of this Power, anything they could find out about it. But each scout returned empty-handed. No one knew what the Power was, or where, or who held it.

Then, weeks after they had first sensed its strength, the scout Herat'lat returned to M'arr. She had an interesting tale to tell.

"I overheard a band of UnderWorlders," she explained to the Fluidmorphers as they gathered eagerly around her. "They were grumbling about the Mipedians. One of them wore robes instead of armor, and he was complaining the loudest. He talked of some object the Mipedians had found, and how it could mean the death of the rest of them. Apparently the Mipedians are unwilling to share it, or even allow the others to see it."

"That is it," M'ahadil stated, his shoulder tentacles waving wildly about his head from excitement. "The object must be the source of the Power we felt! And it belongs to the Mipedians!"

"Yes, but what good does that do us?" another Fluidmorpher, a stout female named Rayan'tar, pointed out. "They are not even willing to let the other three Tribes see it, whatever it is. There is no way they would allow us near it, even if they knew of us!"

M'ahadil grinned at her, his wide lipless mouth

stretching his face and making his gills flap on either side. "Who says we will ask for permission?"

In the end, none of the other Fluidmorphers were willing to take the risk. "We have no idea what the dryland world is like!" they argued. "How can we possibly venture up there? What if we freeze, or burn, or dry out? What if we are caught?"

"If we want to know more about this object, we must go to it," M'ahadil pointed out. "And if the rest of you are too afraid to do so, fine. I will go by myself!" And he flapped his back fins and glided away, leaving his fellows behind to shake their heads and make excuses for their cowardice.

One M'arrillian followed him, however. "I can show you the way to the Mipedian Kingdom," Herat'lat offered, swimming easily beside him. "They live in a desert, but there are streams that emerge there nonetheless. One pours into a small pond not far from their largest city."

"That is where I need to go," M'ahadil agreed. He studied his companion for a second. "But why help me? You've already done your job."

Her body rippled in a shrug. "I want to know what this object is," she admitted. "And I admire your courage. Being a good scout means taking risks, too."

M'ahadil nodded and let her take the lead. Together

they floated along one of the warmer, ascending currents, swimming out of M'arr and across the Deep Ocean, toward the lands of Perim. M'ahadil was frightened by the enormity of his task, but he refused to let that stop him. The other Fluidmorphers were too set in their ways, too afraid to take a chance. He would show them he was right!

It was a long journey, first into the UnderWorld and then up a long, winding underground river, following it as it slid through caverns and mountains. Then finally up through sandy soil and into the waters under the Mipedian Desert. But at last the water around them grew light again, and M'ahadil and Herat'lat emerged in a small pool, the sun beating down on them through its shallow, muddy waters.

"We are near the city," Herat'lat explained, her head near his own so she could whisper. The water carried her soft words to him as gentle ripples. "But how will you get there from here?"

M'ahadil shrugged. "The drylanders manage it," he said, trying to project more confidence than he felt. "So can I."

"There are some now!" she said, and gestured with one tentacle. M'ahadil followed her motion, and froze as they beheld Mipedians for the first time.

“Is that how they appear?” he whispered. “They are so . . . rigid! Their bodies are all angles and edges! And they are scaled like fish!” Like most M’arrillian Fluidmorphers, M’ahadil himself had greenish-gray skin, slick and sturdy and slightly spongy to resist the pressures of the Deep Ocean and prevent damage during collision or Attack.

“Much like fish, yes,” Herat’lat agreed. “Though they are less angular than the UnderWorlders or the Danians. The OverWorlders are the most like us, at least in that they have softer edges and flowing hair much like our strands and tentacles.”

“Hmm.” M’ahadil studied the Creatures above. “Yes, I see. Very well, I can work with that appearance.” The water rippled and sloshed as the Mipedians dunked jars and baskets and bowls into the pool, then settled again as they finished and moved away. After several minutes with no more motion, M’ahadil judged it safe to begin his ascent.

“I will wait for you here,” Herat’lat told him, swimming down to the base of the pool and wedging herself into the space where the underground river flowed up into it.

“Thank you.” M’ahadil tensed, then forced his body to relax. He swam up to the surface, peering at the pool’s edges through the thin layer of water. He did not see anyone around. Finally he gathered his Power to him, drawing upon it to wrap the water tightly around him, and then heaved himself up through the pool's surface.

M'arr's waves, it was hot! Used to the calming chill of the Deep Ocean, M'ahadil was unprepared for such direct exposure to the sun. He could feel his skin boiling and drying to a crisp as the sun's rays beat down upon him. Instinctively he gathered more water, dragging part of the pool up and around him, and turned it to ice, providing a cool shield from the heat and the light. There, that was better!

Blinking furiously, M'ahadil forced his eyes to adjust to the glare. Everything was so bright, and all the edges so crisp! It hurt him to look at them—he kept expecting things to move, to shift subtly with the waves and currents, and when they didn't, it made his head throb. But he did his best to ignore all that.

Glancing around, he spied the Mipedian city. At least, he assumed the collection of strange domes was their city. It was clearly shaped and designed, and held many people, and it was not far from here. Not far by drylander standards, at least—the short distance seemed an eternity to M'ahadil as he contemplated crossing those burning hot sands.

But it had to be done. He considered what he would

need. There was little chance of reaching the object if the Mipedians saw him in his true form, so a disguise of some sort was in order. Fortunately, M'ahadil had already considered that problem during the swim here, and had come up with a solution.

He concentrated on the water he had wrapped around him, and on the ice that hung in a smooth, glittering arc above him. Using his Power, he warmed the ice until it became liquid again, and caught it as it fell about him in droplets and sheets. He draped the water across him like a robe, making sure it covered every surface. Then he began to shape it.

One stream wrapped around his lower body, then encased his two hip tentacles and thickened around them to form a semblance of legs. His torso and arms were close enough that they could pass unchanged, and he forced his shoulder tentacles to stiffen so that they resembled spikes. His back fins became folded wings, and his lower body a tail like what he'd seen on one of the Mipedians by the pool.

The head was the hardest part. M'ahadil's was broad and flat like many of his people, with a wide, lipless mouth and bulging eyes set on either side, and a fin running from the top on down his back. But these Mipedians seemed to have long snouts and teeth, and their eyes perched atop the rest. It was all so strange!

He did the best he could from the brief glimpses he'd had. Then he turned the water dark, masking his true form within its frozen, shaped surface. He would not be able to hold the disguise for long, but hopefully long enough to reach the city, find the object, and at least study it in person.

There was little time to waste, and he set off for the structures, glad that the water around him blocked much of the sun's light and heat. It was all exciting, yet he dreaded the moment he encountered true Mipedians. What if his disguise did not fool them? He was one M'arrillian, alone in a hostile land, trying to find something they did not want others to see. But if he failed, at least he would know he had done his best, not like the others back at M'arr. They were probably still sitting around moaning about how much they'd like to know what the object was! Well, he would find out about it for himself.

Chapter Eight

Much to his surprise and relief, M'ahadil entered the Mipedian city without arousing suspicion. It had helped that, as he'd slogged toward the outermost structures, he had caught a glimpse of several Mipedians going about their business, and had discovered something he had not even considered—clothes! M'arrillians rarely wore garments, and so it had not occurred to him that the Mipedians might. But upon seeing them, and the simple, light cloths they had wrapped around their torsos and waists, he had realized his mistake. Fortunately, someone had hung several such garments out to dry after washing, and M'ahadil was able to grab two of them and sling them about his ice-form. The clothes completed the disguise and covered many of its imperfections, and no one gave him a second glance as he entered the city and walked slowly, carefully toward the large building near its center. It was there, he reasoned, that he would find the object.

M'ahadil moved quickly, aware that his ice-form might not last much longer against the sun's heat. As he drew closer he discovered that the building was in fact a cluster of smaller domes, and so he settled for the nearest of those. But even as he raised his false hand toward its door, he stopped. No. This was not the one.

He tried the next dome, with the same result. He could tell before he'd touched it that the object did not lie within. Nor was it behind the next two.

The first dome of a nearby cluster, however, was different. As his shaped hand neared the door's handle, M'ahadil felt his skin prickle. It was like being near an electric eel, but a thousand times more intense. The object was within!

It took a bit of fumbling to manage the door—he had not bothered to craft full fingers for the disguise, and regretted that now—but at last M'ahadil shoved the door open and stumbled inside. The shade was most welcome, and he sagged against the door as he pushed it shut again.

"Who are you?" a voice demanded from in front of him, and M'ahadil gasped and straightened, both eyes opening wide as he stared. His eyes were still accustomed to the sunlight outside, however, and all he could make out was a corridor before him—and someone standing there blocking his path.

"Who are you?" the figure repeated. "More to the point—what are you?"

Varakarr stared. He had been going outside to fetch some food and water when he'd spotted the strange figure opening the outer door. Every sense had screamed that there was something very wrong about the newcomer, and he had hastened forward, reaching the stranger just as he or she slid the outer door shut behind them. And then he had stopped, aware his mouth was hanging open but unable to do anything about it.

He had no idea what he was looking at.

At first glance, it was a fellow Mipedian, of average height and slender build, with mottled green skin. But the proportions were strange, the skin was oddly rippled, and the face had barely any features. It was more like a bad carving of a Mipedian, but by someone who had only seen them from a distance.

So Varakarr had extended his other senses, humming under his breath and letting his Mugic rise up to grant him sharper sight. And that had been a revelation.

The shape was not a carving—it was a disguise!

Another Creature rode within it, for it was frozen water and its occupant resembled a cross between a snake and a squid. It had tentacles and fins and a long, flowing tail. He had never seen anything like it before.

Now the Creature was staring right back at him, its bulging eyes mounted on either side of its eel-like head. It had power about it, Varakarr could tell that much. He could feel it. Different from his own Mugic, but similar.

"Are you a Muge?" he asked. "What are you doing here?"

M'ahadil stared at the golden-scaled, horned Mipedian in front of him. This one saw through his disguise! But once his shock had faded, M'ahadil could sense the Energy flowing around and through the Mipedian, and he noted that it wore robes with decorated edges and patterns woven throughout. Clearly this was a being of some importance, and some power.

"No," he replied finally, realizing he would have to answer eventually. At least it had not attacked him, or called for guards! "I am not a Muge. I am a Fluidmorpher."

"What's a Fluidmorpher?"

"This." M'ahadil extended one of his hip tentacles and let the water around it shift and reflow, forming the body of a fish. Then he reshaped it into a leg again. Now he had a better example, and the new leg and foot matched that of the Creature before him.

"That's fantastic!" the Mipedian said. "So you're like a Muge, but different. What Tribe are you?"

"I am M'arrillian," M'ahadil answered. He decided there was little reason to lie. And something about the stranger's manner told him talking might be his best option.

"M'arrillian?" the other scratched the spikes that rose from his head. "I've never heard of them. I'm Varakarr. I'm a Muge of the Mipedians."

"M'ahadil," he responded. "I am a Fluidmorpher of the M'arrillians."

"What are you doing here?" Varakarr asked.

"I came to see the object," M'ahadil told him truthfully. "We sensed it, all the way in the Deep Ocean, and I was curious what could contain such Power."

Varakarr considered. He'd never even heard of the M'arrillians—they must be another Tribe, one unknown to the four! That shifted the balance of power completely! And he had come all this way, this M'ahadil, just to see the Sphere? Varakarr knew that Khilai didn't want anyone to see it, or even to learn too much about it, but he didn't agree with her. That was the old, close-minded thinking that had kept the Tribes at one another's throats for so long already. They needed to open up, to trust one another, if they were ever going to change.

He made his decision. "Come with me," he told M'ahadil.

M'ahadil weighed his options. He could try to overpower the Muge and escape, but he had no idea how powerful Varakarr might be. Certainly the reptilian radiated enough strength to be formidable. Yet he had not attacked. Why not?

The Muge had turned away and walked a few paces, then stopped. M'ahadil could see the tip of his tail wagging impatiently. He would have to decide, he realized. Any more delay and Varakarr would lose patience altogether.

In the end, he decided to follow this strange Mipedian. After all, they had exchanged words without conflict. Surely that meant something. If Varakarr were simply leading him into a trap, or to some place where he could be overpowered and restrained, M'ahadil would show them that a Fluidmorpher was a force to be reckoned with. But what if the Muge's intentions were peaceful? He couldn't afford to pass up the possibility.

Struggling to move in both his ice-form disguise and the oppressively hot, dry air, M'ahadil hurried after Varakarr. When he had almost caught up, the Mipedian began walking again, though slowly enough that he could keep up.

Varakarr stopped at a door a short way down the hall. He stared at M'ahadil, hand on the doorknob, and M'ahadil felt as if he were being tested. He forced himself to stillness, and did his best to project an aura of calm and friendship. It was a new and difficult experience for him.

Apparently his efforts were successful, however. After a brief pause Varakarr nodded, though more to himself than to M'ahadil, and opened the door.

The chamber beyond was small and cozy. Rugs covered the floor and the walls, and large pillows were thrown in the corners. Several low tables stood nearby, and one taller workbench was against the far wall, with a few stools drawn up beside it. A strange serpent-shaped staff leaned against the wall not far from the door, and several crystal globes sat upon a polished wooden shelf.

And there, in the center of the room, sat a glowing Sphere atop a thick pillow. M'ahadil could feel it the second he entered. It was like the sun's rays, beating against him all over again, only this time they were mystical waves lapping against him. The object was exerting a powerful pull, and he found himself helpless to resist it. Not that he wanted to.

"We call it the Khilaian Sphere," Varakarr explained, stepping to the side so M'ahadil could approach it. "It was a rock, but somehow it contained immense Power. We shaped it, and focused the Power so it could be used without harm."

"It's incredible," M'ahadil whispered. He dropped down beside it, the limbs of his ice-form shattering and soaking the rugs and pillow, but he only had attention for the Sphere. He reached out, and as his hand came closer, the ice around it melted away until his flesh came in contact with the smooth, polished surface.

Power! The sheer force of it made M'ahadil's entire body spasm, but he wrapped his fingers around the Sphere to avoid losing the connection. Its energy surged into him, filling him, and he could feel himself rising into the air as its song rang within his head. He was floating in the air as if it were water, and turned effortlessly to face Varakarr, who was staring at him, a look of concern on his face.

"Um, I don't think you should—" Varakarr started to say. He'd begun to worry when M'ahadil had knelt beside the Sphere, and that worry had turned to panic when the M'arrillian had picked it up. And now he was floating in midair! This was bad. This was very, very bad. He'd decided to trust his beliefs and go against Khilai's wishes, and he had a sinking feeling he was going to regret that immensely.

"You need to put it back," he told the Fluidmorpher, or started to. But the words never crossed his lips. Instead he saw M'ahadil's eyes flare sun-bright, and then something exploded in his head. The last thing Varakarr saw before he blacked out was the M'arrillian staring down at him—and the Sphere, glowing brightly, held tightly in his grip.

Chapter Nine

M'ahadil studied the Mipedian Muge thoughtfully, though in truth part of him was in shock. How had he done that? The Mipedian—Varakarr—had begun to protest his touching the Sphere, and so he had simply reached out with his mind and—It was amazing!

He could feel the Sphere's power still coursing through him, sustaining him. It was holding him effortlessly aloft. All of his ice had melted or broken away, but he had retained a thin Sheath of water and so he was able to breathe normally, his gills content with even that shallow protective coating. But he had to return to his people! He had to bring them this Sphere, and show them the wonders it could provide for them! He was sure, absolutely sure, that the discovery would change their Tribe forever.

A pounding behind him made M'ahadil start, and he swiveled about, still marveling at how easily he moved through the air now. The noise emanated from the door they had entered before, the one that led to the corridor beyond. And now voices joined it.

"Is everything all right in there? High Mugess? We heard a loud noise!"

The sound of Varakarr hitting the floor, no doubt. M'ahadil scanned the room quickly, but there was no other way out.

Nor did he have time for more than that. The banging resumed, even louder, and then the door slammed open and two Mipedians rushed in. Unlike Varakarr they were garbed in leather straps and strategically placed armor plates, with long curved swords at their sides and even longer spears in their hands.

Guards.

The two Mipedians froze when they saw M'ahadil, and gaped up at him. They recovered quickly, however. "Intruder!" one of them shouted. The other turned back toward the door, his mouth open to repeat that call and summon reinforcements.

M'ahadil knew he could not allow that to happen.

He reached out with his mind again, as he had with Varakarr. The Sphere's music filled him, and he let it carry him along as he engulfed the guards' own thoughts with his own. The first guard's shout died away, and the second clamped his mouth shut before any noise could emerge. Then he turned and faced his fellow again.

I need you both out of the way, M'ahadil thought. *Remove each other.*

The first guard raised his spear, but before he could do more than gesture with it, the second guard charged him, head down. His scaled head slammed into the first one's midsection, sending him flying backward with a loud grunt. The second one followed, but the first guard lashed out with a clawed foot, catching the other alongside his head even as he himself collided with the back wall. The pair sank down onto the pillows there, both unconscious.

Perfect.

M'ahadil flexed his back fins and floated past them and out the door, the Sphere still clutched tightly against him. He was not about to let anything separate him from his prize! He flew quickly back down the corridor toward the outer door, and stretched a hip tentacle toward it, but his mind clutched the handle first and the door swung open for him.

Outside, it was even hotter and brighter without his ice-form, but M'ahadil darkened his water-sheath and continued on, only mildly discomforted. A Mipedian saw him and stopped in his tracks, staring, and M'ahadil froze him with a thought. Others noticed his presence and he stunned them as well, leaving a trail of scaly statues in his wake. They would recover soon enough, he suspected, but by then he would be gone.

"Stop! Who are you?"

M'ahadil turned at the question, to see another Mipedian striding toward him. This one wore robes like Varakarr's, and M'ahadil felt a moment of fear. A Muge! He had caught Varakarr by surprise, but he doubted he would be so lucky a second time. Sure enough, his mind struck out but the newcomer blocked the mental attack with a wave of her hand.

"I asked who you were, and you attack me," she said grimly, Power beginning to gather around her. Her eyes widened. "And you carry the Khilaian Sphere! Very well, thief! Let us see how you fare against an angry Muge!"

She stopped speaking then, and began to sing. The song lashed out at M'ahadil, waves of sound beating against him like an angry storm. But he focused his mind and his Power—and the Power of the Sphere—and the waves parted around him, rippling past without touching him. He could see the surprise on her face as she saw how easily he parried her Attack, but a grimace replaced the look a second later.

"I don't know who or what you are," he heard her mutter, "but you're not getting past me!" She sang again, the melody different this time though there was a similar undercurrent, and M'ahadil could see the strands of Energy emerging from her and reaching toward him. She was trying to trap him!

Frantically he lashed out, and his defense burst from his eyes as beams of light. They cut through the strands, severing them cleanly, and then turned toward her, but she blocked them with a quick word and a glowing disc that appeared before her.

They were well matched, it seemed. But M'ahadil did not have time to linger. He knew the longer he stayed, the more likely other guards would appear, and he was not sure how long the Sphere would sustain him or how many he could control at once. So he concentrated all his Energy on his opponent, and bore down upon her with the full force of his mind and the Sphere's power.

With a small cry, the Mipedian reeled backward. She fell to her knees, her eyes glazed, and M'ahadil exulted. He had won! He struck again, quickly, the same mental tap he had used on Varakarr, and this time she had no defenses left. She crumpled to the ground, her eyes rolling back, and he hurried away from her limp form, hoping he would have at least a few beats before anyone discovered her.

Even in his haste, though, M'ahadil felt a quick thrill. He had faced a Mipedian Muge—their equivalent of a Fluidmorpher! She had clearly been experienced, and skilled. And he had defeated her! Here, in her own city! His respect for the Sphere, and his hopes of what it could mean for his people, rose still higher.

M'ahadil flew swiftly out of the city, stunning anyone who crossed his path. No armed forces rose to block his way, and he did not encounter any more Muges, though after that battle he no longer feared that possibility. But he reached the pool unimpeded, and wasted no time gloating at his victory. Instead he plunged into its shallow depths, rejoicing as the cooler, more immersive waters here replaced his thin water coating.

"Herat'lat?" he called out as he sank down, toward the pool's floor. "Are you here?"

"I am here," the scout replied, unfolding herself from just inside the hole where the river emerged. "Was your venture successful?"

"More than I had dared to hope," he replied, and held the Sphere up for her to see. Its glow shed light all around them.

"It is beautiful!" Herat'lat whispered. Her tentacles

swept toward it, gently, reverently. M'ahadil started to pull it back, then stopped. He had not stolen the Sphere strictly for himself. It was for his people. And without Herat'lat he would never have been able to accomplish that. She deserved to know its touch.

He could sense the Sphere's energy flowing toward her as one tentacle closed the distance, and the spark as she made contact. "Oh!" she gasped, the word bubbling up toward the pool's surface.

"Yes," he agreed. There was nothing more to be said.

"Amazing!" Herat'lat pulled back, and M'ahadil's expanded senses could see the Sphere's glow clinging to her. It faded gradually, but he filed that information away for later. It was not only Fluidmorphers who could benefit by the Sphere's touch, and the effects did not vanish at once.

"We should go," he told her after a beat. "They may be looking for me."

"Of course," she agreed, focusing on their task once more. "Come." She turned and wriggled her way back through the opening, and M'ahadil followed her quickly. They swam down, the Sphere's glow shedding the only illumination as the pool vanished and their way became dark, and its light lit their path as they retraced their steps toward home. M'ahadil could only imagine what the others would think once they saw what he had brought them. He intended to display it to the other Fluidmorphers, but after that, he would present it to the oligarch herself! He was sure Pheren'tal would be pleased.

And then, he thought, *we shall see. We shall see just what this Khilaian Sphere can do for my people. And, if all goes as well as I expect, the rest of Perim will see as well. They will learn of the M'arrillians, and will bow down before our might.*

Chapter Ten

"What—? Oh, no!"

Khilai rushed into her study, the scroll she'd been reading falling to the floor behind her. She hurried to Varakarr first, using hands, eyes, and Mugic to examine him. He was alive! Even as she felt for a pulse at his neck he groaned and shifted slightly, wincing.

Sure that he would recover, she moved to the two guards slumped against the far wall. Both of them had bruises already darkening their scales, but she could see the rise and fall of their chests. They had been beaten and knocked unconscious, but they would survive.

But what had happened here? She glanced around, trying to figure that out. The door had been open when she'd returned from the archives, Varakarr was lying in a heap near the center of the room, and the guards were against the wall. Someone had clearly done this to the three of them. But who? And why?

The center of the room—she looked there again, and gasped. The Sphere!

"Varakarr," she hissed, kneeling by her apprentice again, one hand running over the empty pillow beside him as if to make sure her eyes had not deceived her. "Where is the Sphere? Varakarr!"

"Uhhh!" Varakarr groaned again, and clutched his head. "Ohhh!" His eyes twitched, and after a second, they blinked open, though they clenched shut again almost immediately.

"The Sphere," Khilai insisted, sorry to inflict further suffering upon her apprentice but determined to learn what had happened. "Where is it?"

Varakarr managed to whisper. "The Sphere . . . is gone." Then he passed out again.

Khilai was already on her feet. *Gone! No!* She was running for the door and shouting for guards before she had even finished deciding a course of action. At least she had remembered to grab up her staff, the Serpentotem, as she'd rushed past.

"Someone broke into my study," she informed the first guards to reach her. "They assaulted my apprentice and two guards, and made off with a valuable object, a large, round stone. We must get it back!" The guards nodded, saluted, and took off, one toward the outer door and the other back down the corridor. Both were already calling for reinforcements.

There was no time to waste, however. Khilai followed the first guard as he exited the palace. Surely the thief, whoever it was, wouldn't run deeper into the palace? There was too much chance of getting caught. But who would steal the Sphere? The only people who even knew about it were herself, Varakarr, and the other Muges. Even Kehn-Sep had not been told about it yet.

Kehn-Sep! Khilai stopped and turned back toward the door. She had to tell him! He had to know about the Sphere, its Power, and the fact that it had been taken. She could no longer keep him in the dark.

Heading back into the palace, Khilai strode swiftly down the corridors leading to the Mipedian throne room. The grand double doors were open, indicating that the king was seeing his subjects and dealing with any concerns or problems they brought before him, and a long line had formed leading into the room, with guards set there to keep people from rushing the throne or crowding the king and his advisors. Khilai was one of those advisors, however, and so the guards stood aside, lifting their crossed spears to let her pass.

The Mipedian throne room was a beautiful place, pillars shaped like dragons lining the side walls, tiles decorating the floor in an intricate scale pattern, and delicate stained glass forming a similar design in the high domed ceiling up above. Khilai noticed none of it. Instead she strode down the center of the room, past the various supplicants, and headed straight for the raised platform there at the far end, and the ornately carved throne perched upon it.

"Sire," she said as she drew closer, cutting off a Mipedian merchant who had been complaining about some tax or other. "I must speak to you. It is a matter of crucial importance."

Kehn-Sep, ruler of all Mipedim, nodded. "I will speak with my High Mugess," he declared in ringing tones, rising from his throne. "Wait here, and I shall return and hear the rest of your concerns in a moment." He gestured for Khilai to follow him as he stepped past the other advisors and opened a smaller door against the far wall, near the back corner.

Khilai followed her king into the room, one of his private conference chambers. The walls here were polished wood, a rarity in Mipedim, but the floors were covered in rugs and throw pillows much like those in her own study. As soon as the door had been shut behind them, Kehn-Sep sank down onto a large pile in one corner. He absently tugged the Crown of Mipedim from his horned, crested brow and tossed it onto a nearby pillow, rubbing at the scales where the heavy ornament had sat.

"Ah, thank you!" he told her softly, a smile spreading across his crimson-scaled face. "That merchant was boring me to tears!" His wings spread behind him, their tips almost brushing the far walls, for Kehn-Sep was one of the rare Mipedians who resembled their dragon forebears in form. Though smaller, he was no less majestic, a fact that added to his role as king. "Now, what can I do for you, Khilai? You haven't bothered with court functions for some time."

"I know, your majesty, and I apologize," Khilai began quickly. "But this really is important." She took a deep breath before continuing. "I have been busy working on something. A Mugical artifact. An extremely powerful one." She couldn't help gulping. "And now it has been stolen."

"What?" Kehn-Sep had leaned forward when she'd said "Mugical artifact," but now he leaped to his feet. "Someone stole an artifact from you? Who? When? How?"

"I don't know," she admitted. "I was in the archives, researching tales about Mugic involving the mind. When I returned, the door was open, the artifact was gone, and Varakarr and two guards were unconscious within."

"What does this artifact look like?" Kehn-Sep was pacing now, his wings flapping behind him in his agitation, his long, spiked tail waving back and forth as well.

"It's a polished stone sphere the size of a child's head, in mottled shades of black, white, and gray." She shook her head. "I've already dispatched guards to search for it, and the thief."

"How powerful is it?" was the king's next question.

This was the part Khilai had been dreading. "Very." She couldn't look at him, couldn't meet the golden eyes she knew were boring into her. "It enhances the wielder's mental prowess. One of my Muges was able to overpower me with it, with barely any effort."

The loud flap of Kehn-Sep's wings extending again made her look up, and his eyes trapped her own. "How long?" he demanded softly, his words little more than a hiss. "How long, Khilai, have you been developing this Sphere? And when were you planning to inform me?"

"A few weeks," she admitted quietly. "We found the rock, Varakarr and I, in the Stantin Mines. We shaped it and focused it, made it safe to use, but had only just begun testing its potential. I'd planned to tell you once we knew exactly what it could do."

He stared at her for a moment. "I see." Finally he turned away. "Yes, that makes sense." His wings and tail were still twitching, however. "But now we have a problem. Someone is loose in the city with an object powerful enough to let them overpower my High Mugess! This could be a disaster!" Kehn-Sep reached the door again in three quick strides and threw it open. "Peraxis!" he bellowed.

"Sire!" The Mipedian general was at the door in an instant, his large eyes intent above his short triangular snout. He wore full battle armor as always, the overlapping plates polished but the many dents and scratches attesting to their long and frequent use. His heavy hooked swords hung at his side.

"Seal the city!" Kehn-Sep ordered. "A thief has stolen a Mugical artifact from the High Mugess, and must be apprehended at once!"

"Yes, sire!" Peraxis did not ask further questions. He simply turned away and began giving commands to the guards and soldiers around the courtroom. The general was extremely effective, and Khilai knew that the entire city would be locked down tightly within the hour. The only question was, would that be fast enough?

She got her answer only a few minutes later, when a soldier hurried up to report. Peraxis listened intently, then gestured for Khilai to follow him and strode from the room. The king was right behind her.

The four of them hurried from the palace and down one of the broad streets there—a street, Khilai noted with dread, that led toward the oasis just beyond the city's outermost buildings. But she forgot about that when she spotted a pile of scaly flesh and robes a short distance ahead.

"Firizon!" Khilai rushed to the Muge's side, examining her quickly. "She's alive!" she told the general, the guard, and the king, all of whom hovered behind her. "Alive but unconscious—deeply so." She frowned as her Mugic brought more details. "Someone struck her mind, and it shut down in defense."

"The artifact?" Kehn-Sep asked, and Khilai nodded. It had to be!

"Will she recover?" Peraxis asked, sinking to a crouch beside her. "She may have seen who did this."

"I cannot be sure," Khilai admitted. "Her mind is badly damaged. But I will do what I can to help her, for her sake as well as ours." She cradled Firizon's head in her lap and began to sing a Song of Restoration. The Mugic sank into the unconscious Muge, bathing her in a warm healing glow, and slowly Khilai saw her shattered mind knit back together. At last Firizon stirred.

"Khilai?" her eyes fluttered open. "I am sorry! I tried, but it was too strong!"

"Hush," Khilai told her gently. "You did your best. How do you feel?"

"Weak, and badly battered," Firizon answered, sitting up slowly. Khilai helped her as she wobbled a bit. "But I'll survive. Thanks to you."

"What happened?" Peraxis demanded. "Who did this to you?"

Firizon shook her head. "It was like nothing I have ever seen," she told them, frowning. "It was green and gold, and tentacled, and it floated in the air—and it had the Sphere!"

"Can you show us?" Khilai asked. She didn't want to push the recovering Muge too hard, but this was important.

Firizon nodded. "I think so." She began to sing, her voice faltering at first but growing stronger as the Mugic helped restore her further. In front of them an image began to form, and they all gasped as it took on detail, shape, and color.

"What is that thing?" Kehn-Sep muttered.

"I don't know," Khilai said, and the others shook their heads as well. Firizon was right. She'd never seen anything like it before! It wasn't Danian, that was certain, or Mipedian. But it didn't look an OverWorlder or UnderWorlder, either! She stared at the image, studying the pupil-less eyes on either side, the wide lipless mouth, the flat head, the long tentacles at the waist and the shorter ones mounted on the shoulders, the winglike fins on the back, the fishlike spine that ran down its serpentine back—and the way it glowed with Power. "It is a Muge," she said finally. "Or something very like one. Not all of that Power comes from the Sphere. Beyond that, I have no idea!"

"It is a M'arrillian," a voice declared behind them, and they all turned to stare as Varakarr stepped forward to join them. "That is what it said, just before I passed out. It is something called a Fluidmorpher, like their version of a Muge. And it comes from the Deep Ocean."

Chapter Eleven

The ocean! Of course! Khilai studied its image again. That explained the shape. It lived in deep waters! But what was it doing here? And how had it come all this way? Surely it couldn't survive on land!

"The oasis," Peraxis muttered with a snarl. "It's fed by an underground river!" He raced off in that direction, Kehn-Sep and the guard following him. Khilai let them go. She could already tell it was too late. She didn't sense the Sphere anywhere nearby. It was long gone, along with its strange thief.

"M'arrillian," she repeated, rolling the word around in her mouth. Even with her worry over the Sphere's loss, she felt a thrill at the news. An entire Tribe they had never heard of before! Amazing!

Firizon was looking at Varakarr. "It talked to you?" she asked.

He nodded, wincing at the motion. "I caught it in

Khilai's study, holding the Sphere," he explained, his eyes squeezing tight from pain or remorse or both. "I demanded to know what it was and what it was doing there, and it told me. It said its name was M'ahadil, and it was a Fluidmorpher of the M'arrillians. It said it had come all the way from the Deep Ocean because they'd sensed the Sphere." His crest quivered. "Then its eyes glowed, and it felt like I'd been punched in the head by a mountain. When I woke up Khilai was there, and it was gone." He glanced at Khilai quickly. "I'm so sorry."

"It's not your fault," she assured him, though his grimace said he didn't believe her. "You were no match for it, not with the Sphere. I wouldn't have fared any better."

"I certainly didn't," Firizon agreed, running a hand along her jaw.

Just then the guard returned at a run. "High Mugess, we need your aid," he gasped.

Khilai nodded and accompanied him as he quickly retraced his steps, Firizon and Varakarr following as quickly as they could. They found her standing beside a young Mipedian woman frozen in midgesture. Life Energy still pulsed within her, but her eyes were glazed and her chest barely moved with each shallow breath.

"She has been paralyzed," Khilai explained to the king and the general, who stood there as well. "The

M'arrillian used the power of the Sphere to cast a Song of Stasis." She sang a quick dismissal and Peraxis caught the woman as she drooped toward the ground. "She will be fine."

"There's another one down here!" shouted the guard, who had proceeded past them after he'd brought Khilai to the others. Sure enough, they found a merchant a short ways away, also frozen. A pair of boys stood transfixed beyond him, a ball still clutched in one's hand. They had obviously been playing and had simply been unlucky enough to get in the M'arrillian's way.

Khilai restored them all. There weren't any more. The boys had been near the outermost houses. Beyond them was only the desert. And the oasis.

"It must have used the river to swim here," Peraxis decided, slamming one fist against his armored side. "Then it escaped the same way." He turned to face Kehn-Sep. "Orders, your majesty?"

The king frowned. "Cancel the command to seal the city," he decided. "It's too late for that to do any good." He looked at Khilai. "Can you find a way to communicate with these M'arrillians?"

She nodded. "Now that we know they're in the Deep Ocean, we can search for them Mugically. Clearly their Fluidmorphers have power, so they should stand out to our quests. And the Sphere itself will act as a beacon."

"Good. Let me know when you've found them. I want to know if there's any way to reach them, physically or otherwise." He turned and strode back toward the palace, Peraxis falling into step beside him. The guard followed, leaving Khilai, Firizon, and Varakarr behind.

"Does he think they'll return it if we ask nicely?" Firizon muttered, staring at their retreating monarch.

"No, he knows that's unlikely," Khilai answered. "But he has to try." She sighed. "I doubt there's much chance of getting it back at all. And I worry who these M'arrillians are, and what they mean to do with it."

"What can we do?" Varakarr asked her as they began to make their own way back toward the palace.

"We must do our best to locate these Creatures, and the Sphere," Khilai told him and Firizon. "That's our first priority. Beyond that?" She shrugged. "There is little we can do."

"We should tell the Council," Varakarr declared.

"Why?" Firizon argued. "This is a Mipedian concern. It's none of their business!"

But Khilai shook her head. "Varakarr's right," she agreed. "It was one thing not to tell them about the Sphere when it was secure here and we were only studying it. But now a fifth Tribe, one we've never heard of before, has it.

And we've seen the kind of Power it can offer. It's a threat to everyone, and the others will need to be informed."

"I'll tell them," Varakarr offered. "It's my fault, after all."

"No, it's mine," Khilai replied. "I made the decision not to tell them before. And I'm the one who thought it would be safe sitting in my study. It's my responsibility."

They didn't speak further as they walked. Khilai was busy working out exactly what she would say, and dreading the responses she knew she'd receive in return.

Much to Khilai's surprise, her fellow High Muges were far less concerned about any possible danger than they were annoyed that she had lied to them.

"You should have told me sooner," Sonara insisted, hurt and anger gleaming in her eyes as they communicated Mugically. "I thought we were friends, Khilai!"

"We are," Khilai insisted, "and I wanted to! But this was a Mipedian project. You must understand! You'd have done the same thing, if you had discovered it!"

"You're probably right," the OverWorld High Mugess agreed after a second, a small smile touching her lips. "I would have told you eventually, but I'd have studied it as much as possible first."

"Exactly. I always intended to tell you, and then the others as well, but only once we understood how the Sphere worked." Khilai was relieved to see that her friend was no longer mad at her. That was one thing about Sonara—her temper passed quickly.

"I suppose we'll never get the chance now," Sonara said with a sigh and a small pout. "Pity."

"Yes, but what about these M'arrillians?" Khilai reminded her. "They have the Sphere now! They could do horrible things with it!"

"Where, from the Deep Ocean?" Her friend dismissed the idea with a flick of her tail. "I doubt it! No, they'll probably use it to control fish or something."

"One of them came all the way to Mipedim to steal it," Khilai pointed out.

"Yes—just one of them. Why not send an army? Or at least a small band?" Sonara shook her head. "You said it looked like some kind of fish or eel, and it's from the Deep Ocean. What could they possibly want above the water? The Sphere drew them because of its Power, and now they have it. We'll probably never see either of them again. And good riddance!"

Khilai argued further, but Sonara refused to believe there was any danger. "Besides," she said, "even if the Sphere does make one of them strong enough to defeat one of us, so what? There are four of us High Muges, and we each have close to a dozen Muges behind us. And the Citadel of the Elements powers us all. That Sphere of yours may be powerful, but can it compete with the Four Vortices?" Khilai didn't answer, and her friend took her silence for a no. "There, then, you see? If they were foolish enough to leave their cold, icky waters, we'd simply work together to drive them back for good. But I doubt they'll bother."

The other two High Muges said much the same thing, though in a harsher fashion. Both Litik and Gyrantin accused her of trying to craft a weapon to use against them, and said it served her right to have it stolen, but neither of them felt these M'arrillians posed any real threat to them. And all of them agreed that the Power of Kaizeph would be more than enough to defeat anything these strange water-dwellers could throw at them.

Even Khilai's own king agreed with the other High Muges' assessment. "We have received no word from these Creatures," Kehn-Sep told her a week after the theft. "Surely if they meant us any harm, they would have at least replied, if only to threaten us? And if they wanted communication, they would have responded to our invitation to meet. They want nothing to do with us, or our world. Nor can I blame them"—he shuddered—

"as I certainly wouldn't want anything to do with theirs. I am sorry about this Sphere of yours, Khilai, but perhaps it's for the best." He studied her intently. "An item that powerful and dangerous? The safest place for it might be down in the bottoms of the Deep Ocean."

"And what if they try to use it against us?" Khilai insisted. "We've already seen what it can do. What if these M'arrillians mount an Attack, and use the Sphere to paralyze our soldiers, or overpower my Muges and myself—or both?"

"Then we will deal with them," Kehn-Sep assured her. "But we've seen no movement from the Deep Ocean, no sign of trouble, no hint of aggression. They've spent all these years, however long they've been around, without us even knowing they existed. My guess is they hope if they stay quiet enough, we'll forget again. And I, for one, am fine with that."

"None of them will listen!" Khilai raged, tossing a pillow across the room. "They all insist everything's fine, and that we'll never see or hear from the M'arrillians again!"

"Maybe they're right," Varakarr offered quietly from where he was leaning against the worktable. The two of them were alone in her study and Khilai had just told him about her conversation with the king. “Maybe they’ll stay down there and leave us alone.”

“Do you really believe that?” she demanded, wheeling around to face him. “You saw the thief, that Fluidmorpher. You actually talked to it. Do you really think it will leave us alone?”

Varakarr flashed back to his conversation with M’ahadil. “No,” he admitted, unable to look his mentor in the eye. “No, I don’t. I think they wanted the Sphere for a reason, and I think they’ll be too amazed by what it can do to just sit quietly with it.” He flinched, thinking about how easily M’ahadil had knocked him out. “Especially since they know they can overpower us with it.”

“Exactly! But no else will listen! You’re the only one who agrees with me!”

“I know.” Varakarr pushed away from the table and stepped forward, having made a decision. “Khilai, I am so sorry,” he told her, standing in her path.

“Sorry?” She seemed startled, then laughed. “I told you before, it’s not your fault. It overpowered you.”

“I know.” He wrung his hands, but he couldn’t keep lying to her. “But that’s . . . not all of it.”

“What do you mean?”

“I didn’t tell you . . . everything,” he forced himself

to say. "About what happened."

Now he had her full attention, though he wished he didn't. "What happened?"

Varakarr took a deep breath. "I didn't meet M'ahadil—that was his name—in here. I discovered him out in the hall." He looked Khilai in the eye. "And I showed him the Sphere."

"What?" His mentor staggered back as if struck. "Why? Why would you do that?"

"I didn't know!" he told her desperately. "He said he'd felt it all the way in the Deep Ocean, and just wanted to see it! I didn't think it would do any harm!"

"I'd told you I didn't want anyone to know about it," Khilai reminded him, her jaw starting to clench. "You knew that."

"I did," Varakarr admitted. "And I thought you were wrong! I thought we should share the knowledge in order to make people less suspicious! I thought I was helping!"

"Helping?" She stared at him, then laughed again, but this sound was a harsh, dry scrape of disbelief and disgust. "You thought you were helping? You led a complete stranger, a member of a Tribe we'd never even heard of before, directly to the most powerful Mugical artifact we've ever created, and you thought that would help?" Her voice had risen with every word, and the last was almost a screech of anger, hurt, and outrage. "You've given an unknown enemy a weapon that could destroy us all! Are you happy with your help now?"

"No!" Varakarr held up his hands, begging her. "Please, Khilai! I'm sorry, so, so sorry! I didn't know! The minute he touched the Sphere, I knew something was wrong! I tried to stop him! But it was too late! Please, forgive me!"

"Forgive you?" She stared at him as if she'd never seen him before. "Forgive you?" Then she turned her back on him. "No, Varakarr. I cannot forgive you. No one can—not me, not the other Muges, and not Kehn-Sep when I tell him. You betrayed my trust. You betrayed our people. There is no longer any place for you here. Leave now, before I am forced to bind you and summon the guards."

Now it was Varakarr's turn to stare. He couldn't believe what she was saying! He knew he'd been wrong, that he'd done something horrible, and he'd known she'd be angry, but this! He thought she'd turn back around, that she'd reconsider, but her back remained rigid, its spines straight out, jabbing at him accusingly. At last he sobbed and fled, rushing out of the study, down the corridor, and out into the night. He had no idea what the future held for him, but he no longer cared. He only hoped he would not have to endure this pain very long.

Chapter Twelve

"Attack me! Attack me—if you dare!"

M'ahadil floated in the center of the room, a nimbus of pure Power lighting the water around him and casting heavy shadows against the chamber's distant walls. Caught among those shadows, and the light that spawned them, the other Fluidmorphers hesitated.

Finally, Rayan'tar launched herself at him. "You want a fight, you pompous little windbag?" she shrieked, her tentacles flailing as she shot toward him, her cylindrical body like a fang-tipped projectile. "Fine, you've got one!"

Her Power lashed out even as she closed the distance. The water boiled and froze around him, attempting to burn and sear him simultaneously. It was a clever, nasty Attack. If he defended himself from either shift, he would leave himself open to the other.

M'ahadil smiled and raised his right hip tentacle, presenting the Sphere as if he meant to give it to her. The light pulsing from the orb dwarfed even his own radiant aura, and it strobed into a brilliance so great, it stripped every shadow from the room—and cast them all in front of Rayan'tar.

She attempted to stop herself, backpedaling wildly, but it was far too late. Her own momentum carried her into the shadows, and she shrieked as they wrapped tightly around her. The temperature shifts vanished, cut off as the darkness swallowed Rayan'tar and her Power whole.

M'ahadil let her struggle uselessly for a full minute before he released her. When he did, she drifted to the floor, senseless. She would recover. Eventually.

"Anyone else care to test me?" he challenged.

Most of the other Fluidmorphers backed away, shaking heads and limbs. But one did not move, and M'ahadil swiveled to face him.

Teren'kar. The Master Fluidmorpher. Their leader. Second only to Oligarch Pheren'tal in importance among their people.

"You have shown astounding prowess since you returned, M'ahadil," Teren'kar told him quietly, floating slowly closer, his tendrils undulating around him. "Your Power has increased, as has your control. I am impressed." The master was close enough now that M'ahadil could see his diamond-shaped eye clearly. "But do you think you can best me, mind to mind?"

"We shall see," M'ahadil replied. He bowed low to his mentor and master, showing his respect. Then he lashed out with the Power of his mind. He did not use the Sphere directly, drawing only upon his own Powers, though those had been enhanced from contact with it.

Teren'kar blocked the Attack, a glowing mental shield springing up around his many-limbed form. "A fine first strike," he admitted, his tone as casual as if they were discussing a school of passing fish. But even before the last word had faded from their surroundings, he struck back, a mental hammer blow that slammed M'ahadil right between the eyes.

A month earlier, the blow would have flattened M'ahadil, leaving him a mindless husk. Right after his return with the Sphere, he might have survived the Attack, though he would have been stunned and unable to respond.

Now it slid off his own shield with barely a flicker.

M'ahadil saw Teren'kar's eyes widen, and couldn't help grinning. "An excellent counterattack," he taunted his master. This time, when he struck, M'ahadil did not hold back. The full force of his blow drove Teren'kar to the floor, tendrils splaying out to keep him from flattening further, his mental shields shattering in a shimmer of light and tinkle of sound.

"I yield! I yield!" Teren'kar cried out desperately. M'ahadil ceased the Attack at once. The Master stayed pressed against the floor another moment before slowly rising to face him. Then he bowed. "Truly impressive," he murmured.

"Indeed," another voice agreed. M'ahadil turned and bowed as Oligarch Pheren'tal swam toward them. The M'arrillian ruler was as beautiful as ever, her skin a shimmering blue-green, her three eyes like triangular pearls in her oval face, her tentacles long and slender and tipped in delicate barbs. She was exquisite, but her beauty masked a mind as sharp as any in M'arr, and a will stronger than the waves themselves.

"This is the result of the Sphere's influence?" she asked when she had drifted to a stop between M'ahadil and Teren'kar, far enough back that she could eye them both at once.

"In part," Teren'kar agreed. "M'ahadil was always one of my most promising students, but his Power has increased phenomenally thanks to the Sphere." His round mouth pursed slightly as he considered the situation before speaking further. "The Sphere has granted each of us increased Power, and the ability to touch minds. Yet some have drawn from its Energy more than others.

M'ahadil has the closest bond with the Sphere, and has gained more strength from it than anyone—as you saw."

"Yes." Pheren'tal stretched out a tentacle. "May I?" It wasn't really a question.

"Of course, my liege." M'ahadil extended the Sphere toward her, and their tentacles touched for an instant as he transferred the orb to her. The Sphere's Energy reached out to them both, and for a second they were connected. M'ahadil flushed and tried not to show any sign that he had noticed. Such was not his place.

"Ahhh!" Pheren'tal had clearly not noticed the contact. She was far too busy absorbing the Power of the Sphere. A glow had sprung up around her the second her flesh had touched its smooth surface, and now that nimbus intensified. It was almost blinding, yet M'ahadil found he could not look away. Neither could Teren'kar. They both hung there, transfixed, as their ruler grew in Power. They could feel her mind reaching out to them, but both were strong enough to block it. Others were not, and out of the corner of one eye, M'ahadil saw one of the other Fluidmorphers collapse and drift downward to join Rayan'tar's unconscious form.

"Amazing!" Pheren'tal graced them with a beaming smile before allowing the Sphere to float back to M'ahadil's grasp. Her aura dimmed slightly once she broke contact with it, but it was definitely still there—and still brighter than that of many Fluidmorphers, M'ahadil noticed.

"Will this fade?" she asked, extending her tentacles before her to admire her new inner light.

"It has not yet, your majesty," Teren'kar replied. "It seems the Sphere's changes are permanent."

"And was this the case with the drylanders?" That question was directed at M'ahadil, and he answered quickly.

"Not at all, my liege. From what I saw, they could barely tap its Power at all, and only in direct contact." He had been giving this a great deal of thought since his return. "I believe the Sphere's energies are psionic in origin, and so we are more suited to it by nature. We mesh with it more fully, and that is why it can enhance our Power permanently."

"I see." She studied the Sphere again, nodding. "Yes. Excellent." Her eyes shifted up to M'ahadil again. "I will assemble the Chieftains. You will attend me, and expose each of them to the Sphere. Then I shall speak to our people."

"Of course." M'ahadil bowed again as she swam away. So did Teren'kar. Neither of them commented on the fact that the oligarch had given M'ahadil the order instead of the master. Clearly their ranks had changed.

Twelve hours later, M'ahadil floated just behind Pheren'tal's right side as she addressed the citizens of M'arr.

"My people," she called out, her words carrying easily through the water so that every inhabitant heard her clearly. "The time has come for us to take our rightful place in the world! We will no longer be content to hide here beneath the waves! Soon, all of Perim will tremble before us, and we will bend the entire world to our will!"

The people cheered, the vibrations building and cascading into a veritable tidal wave of sound. Pheren'tal enjoyed it for a moment before signaling M'ahadil, Teren'kar, and the Chieftains to follow her. Leaving the people to their enthusiasm, the oligarch and her advisors retreated to one of her private council chambers.

"A rousing speech, your majesty," Chieftain X'arlon commented once they were settled around the central table. "But how do you plan to achieve such a goal?"

"Yes, the drylanders are strong," Chieftain N'elyar agreed. "And they are four Tribes! We are but one! Even with our new gifts, we may not be able to defeat them all!" M'ahadil had held the Sphere as each Chieftain had touched it in turn, and each had gained some degree of its Powers, though none rivaled the oligarch's gifts, or his own.

"We can, and we will," Pheren'tal insisted. "We will take them one at a time. Dominate each one in turn, and put them to work for us, so our forces increase with each victory. They will all fall before us!"

Around the table, heads nodded. Yes, that made sense. The four drylander Tribes did not work together, so it would be a simple matter to face them separately. And with their new Power, the Chieftains and Fluidmorphers could bend the other Tribes to their will, turning them into slaves and lackeys and servants.

"But what of their Muges?" Teren'kar asked. All eyes swiveled toward the Master Fluidmorpher. "From what M'ahadil told us, they are formidable opponents, and could conceivably stand against us, even with our new strength. If they were to band together, they might overpower us, strip the Sphere away, and then drive us back here or destroy us utterly!"

Several of the Chieftains murmured, but Pheren'tal was not concerned. "Their Muges are indeed a matter of concern," she agreed smoothly. "And if they were to act in concert, they might threaten our plans. Which is why we shall not let them." She smiled as the door behind her opened and another M'arrillian entered. "I have a plan, and our first target. Tell them."

The newcomer smiled as she drifted toward the table.

Most of the Chieftains looked confused, as did Teren'kar, but M'ahadil smiled. "There is a place," Herat'lat began, "called Kaizeph. I can lead you to it . . ."

Chapter Thirteen

"Remind me again why we're here," Derien hissed, hopping up to perch on a low stone wall that circled one end of the wide Inner Yard. "This stone is killing my feet, and I'm so cold my scales are turning blue!"

"We're here to make sure the Citadel of the Elements is safe," Ganott replied absently, leaning against the same wall and rubbing his own aching feet as he watched the lightning flicker across the miniature islands of the Storms. "We can put up with a little chill if it means protecting the city, and the Four Vortices."

In truth, he didn't like being there any more than Derien and her soldiers. Nor did he see much need for it. But Khilai had insisted, and Kehn-Sep had agreed. Finding out about Varakarr's betrayal had shaken them both, but Khilai had believed what her former apprentice had said about the M'arrillian thief. She was sure the M'arrillians would attack them, and the king had ordered a patrol to

Kaizeph to allay her fears. Ganott and Biginth had gone along to bring the troops here and spirit them back once they had made sure everything was fine. Hopefully that would be soon.

Ganott was just about to say something else when he felt his crest tingle and a faint melody touched his ears and his mind. Mugic! He pushed away from the wall at once and readied himself, pulling his own Mugic about him. From the corner of his eye, he saw Biginth hurrying toward him, and knew that his fellow Muge had sensed it as well. Something was happening! And whatever it was, the melody was not Mipedian!

The song grew louder, and a glow appeared in the center of the courtyard. It intensified until Ganott was forced to shield his eyes. Then there was a faint pop and the light faded, the music quieting with it.

Ganott was still blinking to clear his vision when he heard Derien curse and start shouting orders. "Soldiers, to arms!" The other Warriors grouped around her, Ganott, and Biginth, weapons raised. Ganott started to ask what was wrong when his eyes recovered enough to reveal the center of the courtyard—and the group of figures now standing there.

"Who's there?" he called out.

"We are friends," a voice replied. The figures

advanced, and one of them raised a hand and sang a quick burst of Song. Light erupted around her, revealing a tall Creature with a long face, flowing hair, and large, brown eyes. An OverWorlder! And a Muge as well!

"I am Tanita," she declared. "Sonara, High Mugess of our Tribe, sent us to make sure Kaizeph was safe." She smiled, revealing wide, flat teeth. "I gather High Mugess Khilai did the same with you?"

"Yes!" Ganott almost sagged with relief. The OverWorlders and Mipedians were often allied, and he'd heard Khilai speak many times of her friend Sonara. "Welcome!" He spread his long arms to include the entire floating city, and laughed. "Please, make yourself at home!"

Tanita grinned, but sobered a bit as another robed figure pushed past her. "Have you searched the city thoroughly?" he demanded. He was powerfully built, more like a Warrior than a Muge, with thick gray skin and a heavy head. A stout horn rose from his nose, and his eyes were wide set to peer around it.

"We have," Derien replied, "but feel free to patrol for yourself."

The newcomer studied her for a second, then slapped a heavy fist to his chest in salute. "Wilrab," he introduced himself. "OverWorld Muge and patrol leader." It was only then that Ganott realized the other Muge had a heavy sword hanging from his belt, and that he was cradling a helmet beneath one arm.

"Derien, Mipedian Elite." Derien returned his salute. "I'll outline our patrol pattern." The two stepped off to one side and began to confer. Tanita shrugged apologetically.

"Wilrab was a soldier before he discovered the Mugic within," she explained to Ganott and Biginth. "He still relates to Warriors better than to other Muges."

"No problem," Ganott replied. He moved closer to her and lowered his voice so the soldiers milling about wouldn't hear. "Do your leaders really think Kaizeph is in danger?"

She shook her head. "No, who could possibly attack a place like this? But they sent us to make sure."

Ganott nodded, but he actually felt less sure than he had before the OverWorlders' arrival. It was one thing for Khilai to be paranoid. But a second High Muge with the same concerns? That made him wonder if they knew something he didn't.

Not far away, Herat'lat led M'ahadil and the others out of the cool waters of the Riverlands and into the shelter of its hills. "There," she told them, pointing toward the snow-filled valley beyond. "There lies Kaizeph!"

They all stared, squinting against the unaccustomed brightness. The bottom of the Deep Ocean was comfortingly dim, while here the river's surface reflected the bright sunlight and nearly blinded them. After a second M'ahadil nodded. "I see it."

The others nodded as well, one by one, as they caught sight of the floating city. Their target was at hand!

"Are you coming with us?" M'ahadil asked Herat'lat, but she shook her head.

"I'll stay here, so I can lead you back again afterward," she explained. "I'm not a Fluidmorpher or a Warrior—I wouldn't be much help in a fight."

M'ahadil suspected she could hold her own, but he didn't argue. She was the only one who knew the route back home, so it made sense to keep her safe. Instead he turned to the others. "Let's go." He floated up from the water, into the air, and began flying toward Kaizeph. The other Fluidmorphers and the Chieftains flew behind him, while the soldiers marched after them.

They reached the city quickly, and M'ahadil smiled as he assessed the situation. The Citadel of the Elements was an impressive structure, but it was exactly as Herat'lat had described it. It would be easy to invade, difficult to defend. Obviously its creators had assumed that no one could ever reach the city to attack it. But they hadn't known about Fluidmorphers!

With a gesture of his arms and hip tentacles, M'ahadil reshaped the ice and snow all around, sweeping it forward and upward. It formed a long, glittering ramp straight from the soldiers' feet to the edge of the floating city. The M'arrillian troops wasted no time marching up it, and broke into a run when they had covered half the distance.

Which was good, because that was just about when M'ahadil saw a head peek out at them from one of the broad, arched gateways.

"Intruders!" a soldier shouted, and Ganott started, glancing around. He wasn't even sure if the speaker was Mipedian or OverWorld, but it didn't matter. All that he cared about was the response to his question:

"Where?"

"To the south beyond the Wave Gate, and coming fast!" the soldier replied as troops from both Tribes began running in that direction. "I've never seen anything like them! They look like fish, or squids! Or both!"

Ganott glanced at Biginth and Tanita. "M'arrillians!"

"Get ready!" Wilrab hollered. "Stop them from entering the city!"

Ganott was still halfway across the courtyard when

the first M'arrillian reached the Wave Gate. All he caught a glimpse of was tentacles and feelers and scales before the soldiers there jabbed at it with their spears and it fell back and off whatever it had used to reach this height. Another one took its place, however, and more teemed up behind it.

The soldiers were ready, however, and not just with spears and swords. Ganott smiled as he saw Derien step to the front, her hands extending before her. A blast of Air burst from them, intensifying as it crossed the distance and swept a row of M'arrillians off their perch and into the frigid night. Every Mipedian had some access to the powers of the Air, and clearly Derien possessed more than most. With her and her Warriors prepared to use Air and edge against the invaders, he felt sure the Attack would be easily repelled.

A flash of movement higher and to one side caught his eye, and Ganott turned. There was another M'arrillian, but this one was floating in midair! As he watched, it glared down at one of the lead Mipedian soldiers, and a piercing light shot from its protruding eyes. The soldier stiffened, and his scales turned a deep, dark red. Then he turned around—and began attacking his fellow Warriors!

"What are you doing, Maranq?" Ganott heard one of them ask. "The enemy's that way, remember? Stop joking and—*urk*!" The second Mipedian fell, and it became clear that Maranq was not joking.

Ganott was close enough to see Maranq raise a hand toward the other Mipedians, fingers stiff and palm out—jagged shards of ice burst from his flesh! The sharp, frozen spikes slammed into his fellow Warriors, digging deep, and several of them staggered back, crying out in pain. Ganott stared. An Ice Attack? He'd never seen a fellow Mipedian use such a thing!

Biginth had also watched, stunned, and he understood the situation first. "They've taken control of his mind!" he shouted. "He's the enemy now! Stop him!"

There was a pause among the other Mipedians, broken only by grunts and cries as they tried to block their friend's frantic Attacks with blade and ice. It was obvious they were hesitant to attack their comrade, but he showed no such compunction. Fortunately the OverWorlders came to their rescue. One of them, a tall fellow with beautiful blue plumage, stepped in close. He blocked Maranq's ice shards with a disc of Fire, melting the Attack in an instant and sending the dazed Mipedian stumbling backward. While Maranq was still off-balance, the OverWorlder lunged forward and struck him with a solid blow across the head and shoulders. Maranq slumped, unconscious, and the OverWorlder shoved him into the approaching M'arrillians, driving a handful of them back as well. That led to a second pause before the Mipedians started fighting again. Ganott guessed they'd realized they couldn't blame the OverWorlder for defeating their friend, especially when they hadn't been able to attack him themselves.

The M'arrillians were still coming, more soldiers appearing atop what Ganott now saw was some sort of ice bridge. And floating above them were several of what he could only assume were Fluidmorphers, their version of Muges. They were all glowing, and every time they struck a soldier with one of their glowing eyebeams, that Warrior turned against his own friends and allies.

Ganott frowned. "We have to take down those Fluidmorphers!" he shouted to Tanita and Biginth. They nodded. But how?

It was Tanita who suggested an answer. "We need a Cascade Symphony!" she called out. Ganott stared at her for a second, feeling his crest rise and a smile cross his face. Of course! Why hadn't he thought of that?

Together the three of them raised their voices, each singing a different melody but weaving them all together. Wilrab saw what they were doing and joined them, lending his deep, rough voice to the mix as well. Their mingled Mugic rippled out from them in waves, flowing through the air and beyond the city's walls, the sounds cascading as they crashed into one another and resonated together. The resulting symphony struck the floating Fluidmorphers and sent them flying like wisps in a strong wind, driving them far from Kaizeph as they tumbled away uncontrollably. Yes!

But was it enough? Ganott wondered as they ended their song and glanced around. They had removed the Fluidmorphers, temporarily. But the troops were still there, and some of their own people were now fighting against them, creating confusion and hesitation among the ranks. Already their remaining forces were outnumbered. If the Fluidmorphers returned . . .

"We can't hold them!" Wilrab stated, voicing what they were all thinking. "We don't have enough troops to defeat them!"

"We have to save the city!" Biginth insisted. "If we can't do it by force, we'll have to use Mugic!"

But how? They each considered the problem, and then Ganott raised his head. "We have to move it," he informed his fellow Muges. "We have to move Kaizeph."

"What?" Tanita started to protest. Wilrab silenced her.

"He's right," the gray-skinned OverWorlder stated. "If we can sweep the M'arrillians back onto their ice bridges, then break the bridges and move the city, they won't be able to get to us. We can hold off the Fluidmorphers ourselves. It's the only way."

Biginth nodded. "It's better than losing the city to them," he agreed. "Let's do it." He started back toward the Wave Gate. "Wilrab and I will drive the M'arrillians out and destroy their ice bridges. You and Tanita be ready to move the city."

Ganott nodded. He and Tanita moved quickly into the center of the courtyard, right next to the Tower of the Air. That would be the best place from which to make the attempt. But he worried that the other two Muges would not be able to destroy the bridges alone. Especially when he saw a glowing figure soar up beside one window, glaring down at them with a single, round eye. The Fluidmorphers had returned!

Chapter Fourteen

One of the Fluidmorphers, a strange, angular Creature with three glowing eyes arranged in a triangle near the center of its elongated form, turned its gaze upon Ganott. A glowing beam shot from those three eyes, and Ganott raised his hands before his face even as he shouted out a Song of Warding. The Attack struck him hard, but his Mugic took the brunt of it and he staggered but remained standing. For now.

Inside, the Mipedian Muge was trembling, though he refused to show such weakness before his enemy. So strong! He remembered when Khilai had shown all of them the newly fashioned Khilaian Sphere, and had allowed him to test its might against her own mental defenses. She was their High Mugess, the most powerful of their Tribe, yet he had breached her shields easily. He had felt so powerful. But he was sure even that strength would have been nothing compared to the Energy he could feel pouring from the Fluidmorpher he faced. How could he hope to stand against such a being?

The Fluidmorpher struck a second time, and Ganott warded himself, but he could feel his mental shields weakening. Another blow like that would finish him. And then what? Become a puppet for the M'arrillians, like those poor soldiers? Never!

For the third time the Fluidmorpher directed its trio of eyes toward him. But before the fatal beams could emerge, a wave of Energy struck it. The Energy circled the M'arrillian, wrapping around it tightly and forming a glowing cocoon. The Creature dropped from the sky, and disappeared from view.

Ganott gaped. He had been saved! But by whom? The last-second Attack had struck from in front and above the Creature, which meant it had been behind and above him. He glanced back over his shoulder, craning his neck, and saw the Tower of the Air.

And the lone figure standing upon the platform there, radiating Power and fury.

The newcomer wore a heavy, hooded cloak, but the wind pushed back its cowl. The thin, wintery sunlight reflected off golden scales and a proud crest, and Ganott gasped. Varakarr!

Biginth had seen the new arrival as well. "What is

that traitor doing here?" he snarled, eyes narrowing to slits.

"Saving my life, apparently," Ganott snapped back. "And right now we can use all the help we can get!"

His fellow Mipedian grunted at that but couldn't deny the truth of it. They were badly outnumbered, Fluidmorpher to Muge. Any additional help was a gift they could ill afford to refuse. Instead of arguing further Biginth turned his attention to another Fluidmorpher and began attacking it instead, thrusting all of his anger at the airborne M'arrillian in coruscating darts of Mugical Energy.

Ganott grinned and targeted another Fluidmorpher as well, casting a Song of Darkness upon it before it could turn its glance toward him fully. Now, suddenly, he felt like they had a chance.

Standing atop the platform beside the Air Vortex, Varakarr cast about for another opponent. There! He spied a Fluidmorpher drifting into view beyond one of the outer arches, and struck it with a bolt of Power before it had even noticed his presence. The Mugical Energy spear hit the M'arrillian between its single eye and its wide mouth, and the Creature stiffened and plummeted toward the ice and snow below. Another one out of the fight.

Down below, Ganott and Biginth were also attacking Fluidmorphers. At their side were two Muges Varakarr did not recognize. OverWorlders, by the look of things. Sonara must have sent them here for the same reason Khilai had dispatched his two former colleagues—to make sure Kaizeph was safe. At least his treachery had done one good thing, if it had convinced the two Tribes the danger was real. Varakarr ignored the sharp pang in his chest and concentrated on defeating Fluidmorphers. Now was not the time to dwell upon what his foolishness had cost him. He could do that later. If he survived.

Varakarr struck down another Fluidmorpher, and then tensed as a new foe swam into view. This one had bulging eyes on either side of its flat head, and a wide mouth, and at its waist were long tentacles he remembered curling possessively around the Sphere. M'ahadil!

"M'ahadil!" he bellowed, Mugic augmenting his voice so the sound carried beyond the city borders. "Face me, thief!"

The M'arrillian turned, and seemed surprised at the sight of him standing there. Varakarr did not give him time to adjust. He began throwing everything he had at M'ahadil, and his enraged barrage drove him back, battering at his half-raised shields. He could feel M'ahadil's defenses crumbling, and pushed harder. He would have his revenge!

M'ahadil staggered. He had not expected Varakarr to be here—they had not seen him when they'd first attacked—and the Mipedian's sudden appearance had startled him. So had the pure rage he could feel emanating from the Muge. His Attacks, fueled by that intensity, were the most punishing M'ahadil had felt from any drylander, and he could feel them chipping away at his defenses. How was this possible? Varakarr had not seemed that powerful when they had met the first time, and his people were unable to tap the Sphere fully. Nor was it even here! He had left it safely in M'arr. M'ahadil didn't understand, but clearly he would have to find some way to avoid or defeat the furious Mipedian quickly, or he might fall himself, as several of his colleagues had already done.

He blocked another Attack, but a strand of Energy snuck past his shield and sliced through his protective aura. It nicked a shoulder tentacle, and M'ahadil gasped at the sting as his thick flesh parted. Blood began to ooze from the wound. He had to end this quickly!

And not just the duel with Varakarr. All around

him, the tide was turning. The four other Muges were methodically downing Fluidmorphers, and without their support, the soldiers were falling to the drylanders as well. They were losing this battle! And if they failed to take Kaizeph, they would not be able to stand against the drylanders and their Muges. Sphere or no Sphere. Its might was awesome, but even that power could not compete with the Energies contained within the Four Vortices. M'ahadil could feel their Mugic vibrating in the air all around him.

The Four Vortices! He stiffened, and took another cut as his attention wavered. That was the answer! Quickly he turned and hurled a shower of snow and ice at Varakarr. It was a weak Attack, incapable of inflicting real harm, but the flurry distracted him and gave M'ahadil time to dart away. He could hear Varakarr's bellow of outrage as he shook off the snow and realized his rival had vanished. There wasn't much time.

M'ahadil flew quickly to one of the other towers that formed the corners of the city, ascending until he could look down upon the top of the open platform there. A wide, glowing pool filled most of the flat surface, and he could feel the swirling Energy within it calling to him, filling his head with its song. He had chosen instinctively, and well. His affinity for Water, the province of all

Fluidmorphers, had brought him here to what he knew could only be the Water Vortex. The source of all Water-based Mugic in Perim.

It was amazing. In some ways, it spoke to him even more than the Sphere. It was beautiful, awful, and inspiring.

Then he reached out with his mind and his Power and stabbed deep into its heart.

Glowing Water and Energy erupted from the pool as he warped its very core. The song that washed over him faltered, its melody shattered, its notes turning sour. Something within M'ahadil cried out in sympathy, but he hardened his heart and continued his Attack.

And the great Citadel of the Elements suddenly tipped to one side, as the power of the Water Vortex flickered in and out and the city lost its balance, both Mugically and physically.

It was working!

M'ahadil continued to disrupt the Water Vortex, and was forced to fling himself backward as that corner of the city plummeted, the tower almost flattening him. He could hear screams and shouts as attackers and defenders alike struggled to hang on while the city tilted crazily. The Fluidmorphers were unaffected, floating safely beyond the city's walls, and resumed their Attacks. The tide was turning yet again—this time in their favor.

But why stop here, M'ahadil thought. He intensified his intervention, distorting the Water Vortex still further and making the entire city careen about the sky. With some careful maneuvering, he realized he could probably control its bucking and spinning, possibly even smash it to the frozen ground below. Then his eyes caught sight of the glittering oval off to one side, and M'ahadil smiled.

Even better.

"Hang on!" Ganott shrieked, clinging to the small wall he'd perched upon what seemed like an eternity ago. "Don't let go!"

"Thanks for the advice!" Wilrab snarled, his stocky frame wedged into a doorway. "We'd never have thought of that ourselves!"

All around them, the battle had turned to chaos. They had been winning, defeating the Fluidmorphers and driving the M'arrillian Warriors back onto their ice bridge, when the ground had suddenly dropped out from under them. Then it had bucked and tossed like a crazed beast, tossing all of them about as they struggled to stay upright and then just not to slide out of the city altogether. Many of their Warriors had been battling near the city's edge, and had fallen, plummeting to the cold ground below. Ganott had no idea if any of them had survived, but right now he had other things to worry about.

Like what had shaken Kaizeph loose from its centuries-old Mugical moorings?

"It's the Water Vortex," Tanita gasped out, her long arms wrapped tightly around a small pillar. "Something's happening to it. Its melody has been corrupted!"

Ganott stared at her. Corrupted? How could anything tarnish the might and purity of one of the Four Vortices? He didn't understand. Then realization dawned, and he wished it hadn't. The M'arrillians! They were Fluidmorphers, attuned to Water and ice. One of them must be interfering with the Water Vortex! And the union of the Four Vortices was what kept the Citadel of the Elements in the air!

Even as he thought that, the city tilted still further, and began to drop like the many tons of stone it was. But not straight down. No, it swiveled and twisted and swayed, rampaging through the sky as it flung itself across the valley below—and directly toward Lake Ken-I-Po.

"Look out!" Ganott had just enough time to shout before they struck.

Water exploded around them as Kaizeph smashed into the lake at a steep angle, its arches and pillars and towers slamming into the ice-cold waves. The distinctive note of shattering crystal pealed out across the water. The city's weight and momentum carried it beneath the surface in an instant, and Ganott felt his perch torn from him as he floated up, flailing in a desperate attempt to reach air once more.

The air! He felt his connection to it shatter, as if someone had torn the Mugic from him and shredded its remains. What had happened to the air?

It was the Four Vortices, he realized. The fall had damaged them all, and shattered the crystal table Varakarr had described after his first visit to the Chamber of the Emperors. A table Khilai had claimed might be involved in amplifying and distributing the Vortices' Power. The city's balance had been destroyed, and the Vortices disrupted. Possibly for good.

But right now he had to worry about surviving. He could figure out what had happened to the Vortices—and how to restore them—later.

Ganott blinked, trying to see through the waves. His lungs were burning. He'd managed to hold his breath as he struck, but his air was almost gone. He needed to reach the surface! There! That glow above him. It had to be the sun. He struggled toward it.

But it wasn't. His heart plummeted as the glow

drew closer, and Ganott could make out the writhing shape within it. His vision began to fade and he gasped involuntarily, choking as he swallowed water. The Fluidmorpher drifted closer, completely at home in the water, and watched him calmly. The last thing Ganott saw was its single eye staring at him, unblinking.

Varakarr had clung to one of the spires that adorned the edges of the Tower of the Air platform when the city had dropped. He'd managed to hold on until he saw the waters rushing toward him, and then had wisely let go and jumped as high as he could. As a result, he'd struck Lake Ken-I-Po half a second after the city did, and the splash its impact created had actually driven him upward so that he hadn't gotten tangled up in its heavy stonework. Now he surfaced and splashed about, looking for his allies. But most of them had apparently not been as lucky.

The M'arrillians who had fallen to the ground back in the valley were streaming toward the lake and diving into it, thrilled to take the fight to more familiar surroundings. Some of them were already emerging with unconscious Mipedians and OverWorlders, tossing their limp bodies up on the banks. He had no idea what the

M'arrillians planned to do with their prisoners, but knew it couldn't be good.

He was still floundering, attempting to reach the lake's edge himself, when a glowing figure breached the water beside him, bobbing gently not ten feet away. A pair of bright bulbous eyes studied him, and the wide mouth pursed in thought.

"Now what shall we do with you, hmm?" M'ahadil wondered aloud. "You're too dangerous to leave behind, and may have something useful to tell us. I think we'll bring you along." His eyes glowed even brighter, and Varakarr found he could not look away. "Come with me." He struggled, but he was already stunned by the city's fall and the Vortices' disruption and his own immersion. His concentration was in tatters. Varakarr opened his mouth to cry out as he felt the Fluidmorpher's mind overwhelm him. Then he fell into a warm, thick embrace, and knew no more.

"Success!" N'elyar swam toward M'ahadil, his face stretched into a fearsome grin. "The city is ours!"

M'ahadil nodded. "More importantly, the Vortices have collapsed," he replied. "The drylanders and their Muges will be powerless."

“What of that one?” N’elyar gestured toward the mind-snared Varakarr, who floated in the grip of M’ahadil’s hip tentacles.

“He may be useful.” M’ahadil smiled. “Gather the troops. We return to M’arr at once to inform the oligarch. The war has begun!”

Chapter Fifteen

Khilai was restlessly rereading an old scroll, trying to force her mind to focus on that instead of her concerns about Kaizeph, the Vortices, the Sphere, and—despite everything—Varakarr. She had just struggled through the same sentence for a sixth time, trying to make the words make sense, when she felt the Mugic all around her, the delicate melody that filled the air and lifted her spirits and her mind—vanish.

"Oh!" The scroll fell from her hands, hitting the floor and her feet with a dull clatter. Khilai didn't notice. She was too busy extending her senses, reaching out for the Mugic.

But it wasn't there.

"No! No, no, no!" Forcing her panic back down and taking a deep breath to control her fluttering heart, Khilai lifted her head, opened her mouth, and sang. It was a simple song, a Hymn of the Elements, meant to draw a comforting breeze.

Nothing happened. Nor did reaching for her staff change anything. The Serpentotem felt dull and lifeless in her grip.

"No, oh no!" She raced from her study and ran down the corridor. "Firizon!" she shouted. "Kirun! Shimo!" She wished, for the hundredth time, that Varakarr was here, but shoved that thought away. He didn't deserve such attention. And right now she had bigger things to worry about.

The other Muges emerged from their chambers, and her heart sank as she saw the confusion and despair written on all their faces. Before they'd even opened their mouths, she knew they had experienced the same loss she had.

It could only mean one thing. Something had happened to the Citadel of the Elements, to Oronir's crystal table, and to the Four Vortices. And that boded ill for them, and for their Tribe in general—in fact, for all of Perim.

Khilai didn't have time to comfort her Muges. She ordered them all back to their chambers for now, assuring them they would speak later and study and look for some sort of solution. But right now she had to inform the king.

"Kehn-Sep!" she shouted as she ran for the throne room. "Kehn-Sep!" The guards moved out of her way and she barreled into the room, then skidded to a stop. There was no one here! Normally the throne room was filled with Mipedians seeking the king's aid in resolving some situation, or complaining about this or that tax, or bringing him gifts to curry favor. But the spacious chamber was empty now, except for a handful of figures clustered at the far end. She recognized the king by his majestic wings, even at this distance, though he was pacing the dais rather than sitting on his throne. The smaller figure marching beside him could only be General Peraxis.

"Your majesty!" Khilai hurried toward them. "Something terrible has happened! The Mugic has vanished!"

Kehn-Sep stopped and turned to face her, and she started when she realized he was wearing his golden armor. It had been iron once, when he had battled for the throne all those years before, and he had plated it with gold after he had won the crown, but she could still see the dents under that glossy finish and knew it was as strong as ever. But Kehn-Sep had not worn it except for parades and military reviews in almost six years.

"I felt the change in the air," he explained to Khilai as she joined him, Peraxis, and the other royal advisors on the dais. "It grew leaden around me, thick and dull. I drew upon the Sirocco to stir the air, but nothing happened."

His wings flapped behind him. "These are all the Air I have left."

"What does this mean?" Peraxis demanded, glaring at Khilai as if she might somehow be responsible. And, in a way, she worried that she was.

"Kaizeph," she answered. "I have heard nothing from Ganott and Biginth. They would have reached the flying city hours past." She sighed. "I can only assume we were correct. The M'arrillians attacked, and destroyed or conquered the Citadel of the Elements. They control the Four Vortices now, and have found some way to sever our bond with those fonts." She shook her head. "Our power is all but gone. We are helpless."

"You may be helpless," Kehn-Sep corrected her, "but I am not!" He reared up to his full height, wings extending behind him, and drew the gleaming broadsword at his side. "I am Kehn-Sep! I battled hundreds to achieve the throne! I conquered the Oasis single-handedly! I battled UnderWorlders by the score, and Danians by the dozen, and defeated them all! I am still king of the Mipedians, and any who challenge me shall feel my wrath!" The last word came out as a roar loud enough to shake the pillars lining the walls, and while they still quivered he turned to Peraxis. "Assemble the army! If the M'arrillians mean to attack us, they will emerge from the pool as they did before! They will find us waiting for them!"

Peraxis began to nod, but before he could speak, Khilai cut him off. "No, they won't!" she insisted. "That was when they needed stealth and secrecy! This is different!"

Kehn-Sep glared down at her. "Then where will they strike us, High Mugess?"

"I don't know," she admitted softly. "But they won't be alone! Remember how their thief froze Firizon and the others like statues? And what the guards said, the ones who came upon M'ahadil and . . . and Varakarr in my chambers? They said they attacked one another, as if their limbs were not their own!"

The king was still scowling, but Peraxis rubbed the bridge of his wide snout. "You are saying they can control others, and turn them into slaves?"

"Yes! And I fear they'll have grown better at that since they stole the Sphere."

The small general was frowning now as he considered this new information. "If that is true," he said finally, "Khilai is right. They will not emerge from the pool. They will march across the sand—and they will have the Danians at their fore."

"The Danians!" The king all but spat the name.

"Yes. If they can truly subjugate others' will, they will confront the Danians first." Peraxis shrugged. "Individually the Danians may not be as strong as OverWorlders or UnderWorlders, but they possess vast numbers. And they are a Hivemind—that may make it easier to control them." He glanced at Khilai and she nodded. She had never had a reason to attack a Danian's mind, but judging by those she'd dealt with, their thoughts were tightly regimented and they were accustomed to taking orders. They would be far easier to dominate than any of the other Tribes. "It is what I would do, if I were them," Peraxis concluded.

Kehn-Sep glowered at him as well, then nodded sharply. "Very well. Assemble our warriors and prepare them to march." A grim smile touched his lips. "We confront the Danians! If necessary, we will conquer them ourselves, and keep the M'arrillians from turning them against us."

Peraxis nodded, saluted, and marched off to deliver his orders to the commanders waiting a respectful distance off to the side. The other advisors shrank back, leaving Kehn-Sep and Khilai alone on the dais.

"Will the Mugic return?" the king asked, idly slashing the air with his blade.

"I do not know," Khilai admitted. "We don't know what they did to the City, or to the Vortices. It might. We might regain some of it, but at a lesser level. Or . . ." She could not bring herself to voice the other possibility—that the Mugic might be gone forever.

"I hope it returns," Kehn-Sep said so softly she almost didn't hear him. "I miss the feel of the Air caressing my skin." Then he shouldered past her, hopping off the dais with a short beat of his wings, and strode from the room.

"I hope so, too," she whispered after him. "For all our sakes."

Chapter Sixteen

"They come."

The simple pronouncement carried through the halls, echoing through the vast, empty chambers. Litik shuddered.

Beside him, Ibicara stood slowly. The queen of the Danian Hive was no longer young, though she still possessed good health and enough Energy, passion, and will to control their entire Tribe. Her slow progress was less a sign of infirmity than a mark of the sorrow and even fear that gripped her, and all their people.

Raising her diamond-shaped head, Ibicara's large, faceted eyes studied the few who stood near her. Litik was there, as was his right as High Muge. On her other side stood Virinil, the Danian Warlord and master of the queen's legions. Two of Litik's Muges stood behind him, and two of Virinil's commanders attended him as well. A few paces directly behind the throne stood Gimitin, one of the leading Danian nobles and the queen's consort.

The rest of their people waited in their dens and burrows, listening for the queen's summons.

"Is there nothing you can do?" she asked Litik, turning toward him. He shook his head silently. With the Mugic gone, he had no more power than a Mandiblor, and far less muscle.

"Very well. Then we must face them through strength of arms, and of numbers." Her antennae quivered as she raised her voice. "To me, my people! Rise up and defend our home! Fight for your Tribe, your Hive, and your queen!"

A loud buzz and hum answered her summons. Throughout the massive Hive, the Danians heard her call and responded. Mandiblors, Squad leaders, Battlemasters, and Nobles all rushed into the central chamber, flying and hopping and crawling and marching as best they could. The enormous space filled quickly, as thousands upon thousands of Danians obeyed their queen and gathered around the central platform where she and her advisors stood.

"We are faced," she told them once they had assembled and settled slightly, "by a threat like no other in our history. A fifth Tribe, the M'arrillians, has emerged from the Deep Ocean. They have sunk Kaizeph, the legendary

Citadel of the Elements, into Lake Ken-I-Po and crippled our Muges in the process. Now their soldiers come for us. They seek to destroy us and our homes. But we will not let them!" The answering hum vibrated throughout the hall. "We will fight back! We will show them what it means to invade the Danian Hive!" The hum grew louder, and the very walls shook. "We will teach them to fear our might!"

With a roar, Virinil leaped into the air, his wings unfolding behind him and carrying him higher in a blur of shimmering blue. "For the Hive!" he shouted, raising his sword high in the air. "For the queen!" The answering shout nearly tumbled him from the air, but he righted himself and flew swiftly toward the chamber's exit. His commanders had risen behind him, and now began calling orders to their Battlemasters, who organized their squads and set them to marching. Soon the Danian army was on the move, heading for the Hive's exit and the plains beyond.

That left the Mandiblors, lowly workers and guards, and the helpless Muges. "To you, my loyal subjects," Ibicara told them, "has fallen a great and terrible burden. For you must defend me, and our home, in case these M'arrillians seek entrance here. You must prevail against this foe, and hold them off until the armies can come to your aid. Will you take on this momentous task?"

Their eyes shone as every Mandiblor dropped to one knee and vowed to defend the queen with his life. Litik couldn't help being impressed. His queen had always had a gift for making every member of the Hive feel valued and respected.

A short time later, however, he wondered if she had somehow seen the future. Because he and the other remaining Danians all jumped when they heard a strange crackling noise from the front entrance to the Hive. A terrible tearing sound followed that, and then a wave of green and gold Creatures floated, crawled, and slithered into the chamber.

M'arrillians!

They really had come here, Litik realized as he grabbed a spear leaning against the far wall. He might not have his Mugic but he could still offer life and limb to protect his queen.

Even that proved useless, however. One of the M'arrillians, a long, snakelike Creature with a ring of eyes set around its circular mouth, flew toward them, the glow of its curving body lighting the entire hall. It hovered before the central platform, regarding Litik and the others, before its gaze fastened upon Ibicara.

"You will not have my queen!" Litik declared, hurling the spear at the invader. But a wave of Energy erupted from the Creature, and the spear was knocked aside. It clattered onto the floor below but the M'arrillian never lifted its eyes from the queen.

She met its strange gaze proudly, lifting her head high. "I am Ibicara, Queen of the Danian Hive," she declared in rich, ringing tones. "Depart at once, or face my royal wrath!"

The M'arrillian said nothing.

They glared at each other for a moment, neither one moving. Then light burst from the Creature's many eyes, a dozen or more narrow beams that met a short distance past its mouth and merged into a single, wider beam—which shot toward Ibicara and struck her full in the face.

Litik watched, frozen in horror, as his queen struggled against the Attack. She was no match for the M'arrillian, however, and after a second her body stiffened and her eyes glazed over. The beam winked out, but Ibicara's eyes continued to glow on their own.

And then Litik felt her through the link he and all Danians shared. Only then did he realize the true cunning of their foes. They had known about the Danian Hivemind. They knew that all Danian minds were connected. And so they had struck here, dominating the queen who was their center, their focus. And through her, they could control all the rest.

Litik fought against the blankness that swept through him, but he knew it was no use. Even with his Mugic, he would not have been able to withstand it, especially since his bond with the queen bypassed all of his mystical defenses. He could feel himself losing control, and then his consciousness was swept away.

Out on the battlefield, the Danians stopped fighting. All of them stood immobile for a second. Then they straightened, and moved quickly into orderly ranks. They were ready for battle once more, ready to go wherever and fight whomever their queen—and, through her, their new M'arrillian overlords—commanded.

Within minutes, the Danian army was on the march. And they were headed straight for the desert—and the Mipedian Kingdom nestled within it.

Sinking down onto the pillows scattered about her chambers, Khilai tugged angrily at her crest. There had to be something she could do!

A faint stirring in the back of her head made her glance around quickly. It had almost felt as if someone were nearby. But she was alone. After Kehn-Sep's departure she had decided she needed a few minutes to herself, just to calm down and organize her thoughts.

But still the sensation that someone was present persisted.

Frowning, Khilai forced her eyes closed and took deep breaths, attempting to relax. Perhaps if she could settle into meditation, that would help clear her head and open her senses. Out of reflex she began to hum, a simple melody of focus and concentration—and leaped to her feet as she felt the song echo in the air around her!

The Mugic was back!

It was faint, however. So faint she was still not entirely sure she hadn't simply imagined it. Clearly the Mugic was struggling to return, but whatever the M'arrillians had done to Kaizeph had damaged it severely. She also suspected they had destroyed Oronir's crystal table, and she had no idea what sort of consequences the loss of that artifact might produce. Still, just the fact that all Mugic had not been permanently destroyed made her heart sing with joy.

Now, how could she use its return?

The Mugic was too weak to sing any true songs, she could tell that at once. And it could not sustain their own abilities as well, though she hoped that might change. Having access once again to Attacks like Windslash and Tornado Tackle would make a tremendous difference for Kehn-Sep and his Warriors. But how could she help them?

Khilai considered. If she couldn't grant them protection, or vanquish their foes, perhaps she could at least provide information. And perhaps allies as well.

Closing her eyes again, Khilai concentrated. The echo had seemed stronger to one side of the room than at its center. Why? Blinking, she looked in that direction—and gasped. The crystal orbs! Their shelf was there, right where the Mugic had felt the strongest! Each sphere contained powerful Mugic of its own, and was linked to a Muge's spirit. Could those have retained some of their strength, perhaps because the crystals served as a protective barrier?

Hurrying across the room, Khilai touched the nearest orb. Yes! She could feel the Mugic within it! She ran her fingers along them. With these she still had at least a few songs at her disposal. Would they be enough?

Well, they would have to do. She selected one, a sharp-edged crystal with a pale green hue, and reached out to it, trying to draw upon the Mugic within. But her will was not enough. She would need help to breach the crystalline shell.

Fortunately, there was aid at hand. Khilai smiled as she felt the presence beside her. She recognized it at once. It was the last traces of Maranac, her master and mentor.

"Thank you, Reldiar," she whispered. And she

thought she felt a wave of warmth and affection in return.

Then she surrendered her will to him. Her spirit joined with his for that instant, and together they pierced the crystal. It began to glow, and that aura intensified as the Ember Flourish inside it burst forth.

The song was soft at first, the Mugic barely stirring, but it grew in strength until Khilai was sure she could hear the Energy rippling and dancing and vibrating around her. Once it was attuned, she cast out with her mind, searching for the OverWorld aura she knew as well as any of her own Muges—the one person she could trust to recognize the aria and accept the link it offered.

"Sonara," she called, projecting the name through the song and using it as the Mugic's target as well. "Sonara!"

On the opposite edge of Perim, she thought she felt a faint response. The song was still faltering, but Khilai concentrated on maintaining it, and sang louder. This had to work!

At last she felt the response again, stronger this time. Then it latched on to the aria, as a distant, velvety voice began to sing in time with her. Relieved, Khilai finished the song, their two voices woven together, and the Mugic wove them together as well, bridging the distance.

With the last note still hanging in the air, Khilai opened her eyes—and smiled as she met the almond-eyed gaze of her friend Sonara, who was peering at her from a floating disc of light.

"Khilai?" the OverWorld High Mugess asked. "Is it really you? Has the Mugic returned?" Sonara's tail twitched behind her, and her whiskers quivered eagerly.

"Only the tiniest bit," Khilai answered, sorry to have to dash her friend's hopes. "You will need to use your orbs, the ones the Muges before you left behind. Join your spirit with theirs to access the Mugic within them. At least it is something. And hopefully in time the rest of the Mugic will return as well."

Sonara nodded. "When I felt the melodies vanish, I knew something was wrong. And I have had no word from the troops we sent to Kaizeph."

"You sent troops there?" Khilai smiled. "So did we. But we have heard nothing, either."

"The M'arrillians." Sonara spat the name out.

"I believe so."

"What can we do?"

Khilai sighed. "I don't know," she admitted. "Kehn-Sep has assembled his warriors and is marching to our border. We fear the Danians may attack—because the M'arrillians will be controlling them." She explained her theory.

"That makes sense," Sonara agreed. "Though I wish it didn't. All those Danian Warriors, under M'arrillian control? Brr!" she shivered, the chill rippling her glossy fur. "I can speak to Yerek about sending some of our Warriors to aid you."

"Would you?" Khilai sagged with relief. "That would be—" Before she could finish expressing her gratitude, however, Sonara stiffened. Her ears swiveled back, and then she turned, tail lashing as she spoke with someone Khilai could not see. When she swung around to face Khilai again, her eyes had narrowed and her tail was puffing out.

"Our scouts have just brought word that the UnderWorlders are marching on us," Sonara explained. "Their entire army. It is a full-scale invasion!" She shook her head. "I am sorry, Khilai. Yerek will need all our forces to confront the UnderWorlders."

"I understand." Khilai couldn't help the chill that washed over her. "It may not be the UnderWorlders' fault," she pointed out. "Dyragar is no fool, and he wouldn't start a war with you when he knows the M'arrillians could attack at any time. They may have already conquered him."

"I know. But either way, our Warriors will have to face them." Sonara stood. "And I will be there as well."

"You?" Khilai stared at her friend. "But without the Mugic, what can you do?"

"Very little," Sonara admitted. "But I will go nonetheless. If this battle decides our fate, I will be there to lend whatever aid I can."

Khilai nodded. "Good luck," she said softly.

"Thank you. And to you." Sonara smiled briefly, then hummed a note and the song unraveled.

Alone again, Khilai considered her friend's words. Yes, Sonara was right. These were momentous battles, and their place as High Muges was beside their kings. She rose, gathered the remaining orbs, and headed for the door. If she hurried, she might still catch up to Kehn-Sep before he reached the border.

Chapter Seventeen

Sonara stood to the side, feeling helpless. She watched from the small foothill as Yerek, leader of the OverWorld, led his Warriors in a charge across the wide plain. At the opposite end, where the plains ended and the mountains began, figures were still pouring from a wide cavern. Even from this distance, she recognized the two in the lead, the one with gray skin, wide horns, and wings, and the other with bright red skin and shock-white hair and a long, razor-sharp beak. Gyrantin and Dyragar—the UnderWorld High Muge and the UnderWorld Ruler. Shouts arose from them as they spotted the OverWorlders streaming toward them, and they rallied their own troops and began advancing as well.

Normally, Sonara would be here with her Muges, their voices raised to the sky, their Mugic crafting powerful songs to protect their Warriors and assure their victory.

Right now the most she could manage was to call

upon one of her few orbs and sing a weak hymn to protect Yerek himself. And she had no idea if it would help at all. But she had to try.

The two forces collided just past the center. She felt the impact from her perch, and coughed as dust billowed up from the dry ground, the result of so many feet stamping across it at once and then so many bodies clashing together. When the dust settled, she saw Warriors in battle, but she also saw something else, something that made her fur stand on end.

Floating above the scene were several glowing figures in green and gold, wiggling and shimmering like strange fish using the very sky as their pond.

M'arrillians!

It was true, then, what Khilai had told her. The UnderWorlders had fallen under the M'arrillians' control. This invasion was not done freely.

Not that it mattered much. Yerek could not have allowed them to march their army through the Tribe's lands. He had been forced to meet the UnderWorld soldiers here, no matter who was in charge of them.

But it did affect the outcome. Sonara watched as an OverWorld Warrior she recognized fell before an UnderWorld blow—and rose again a minute later. But he seemed different, his movements leaden, his complexion somehow darker. Even from here she could tell that his eyes were glazed and unfocused, and she shuddered. He had been taken over.

Near the edge of the battle closest to her, Sonara saw Zartac, one of the OverWorld's finest Warriors and patrol leaders. He was shouting at an approaching UnderWorlder, brandishing his sword at the tall, spike-encrusted figure, and after a second, Sonara nodded. She had seen the UnderWorlder, Raritage, once or twice before. Those two were bitter rivals, and their patrols clashed frequently.

"At last we will settle our differences, Raritage!" She could hear Zartac shout. "With blood!" He leaned his head back and roared, his mane billowing around his face.

But the UnderWorlder did not reply. He just kept advancing.

"Oh, are you too good to face me?" Zartac snarled. "Or too much of a coward?" That also got no reply, and Sonara could see that the lack of response puzzled Zartac. "Fight me, Raritage!" he roared. But Raritage did not even acknowledge his presence.

At last, with a wordless cry, Zartac leaped into his rival's path and swung at him. Raritage blocked the blow and lashed out with one claw, and the two began to fight. But it was a strange conflict, the OverWorlder shouting and cursing and the UnderWorlder eerily silent. Raritage also seemed unusually strong, judging by how easily he caught Zartac during one leap and hurled him back one-handed.

The changes in his old foe clearly shook Zartac, as did the pummeling. His blows became more desperate, and sloppier, and after one swing that went wide of its mark, Raritage simply caught him by the throat and squeezed. He dropped the limp OverWorlder to the ground after a few seconds—and an instant later Zartac was on his feet again. But now he turned and paced shoulder-to-shoulder with Raritage, sword raised against his own people.

It was too terrible to watch. Sonara turned away, covering her face, ashamed that she could not spare her people this horror. The sounds of battle still reached her, but after a time—a surprisingly short time—they stilled.

Cautiously, she glanced around.

The battlefield was still filled with Warriors, but there was very little fighting left. Most of them stood silently, OverWorlder and UnderWorlder together, weapons held at their sides—and faces turned up to the sky.

Or to their new overlords, hovering there.

A sound nearby made Sonara turn, and her own eyes widened as a glowing figure descended only a few lengths beyond her reach. Its four eyes waved above its head like a grotesque crown, and its small, round mouth was pursed in what she somehow knew was a nasty grin. Then its eyes flared brighter, and Sonara felt her own mind being overwhelmed.

It was almost a relief to let the darkness claim her.

Khilai had run as fast as she could, regretting the loss of her Mugic with every stumble and every gasped breath. But she had caught up with Kehn-Sep and his Warriors at the edge of their Tribe's lands, while the soldiers were still arraying themselves across the wide stretch of sand. Just beyond that point the sand gave way to dirt, and then loose scrub beyond, followed by trees and vines. Somewhere beyond that tangle lay the mountains beneath which the Danians nested. If they were attacking, it would be from that direction.

The king glanced at her as she reached him, one brow raised.

"I may not have any Mugic," Khilai told him between breaths, "but I am still Mipedian, and I will defend our home with my life." She chose not to mention the orbs yet. The Ember Flourish had been so weak she was not sure the others would yield any results at all, and she did not want to get his hopes up.

The nod Kehn-Sep gave her was deep, and she thought she saw the hint of a smile tug at his lips before he turned away to confer with Peraxis. Kehn-Sep's acceptance of her decision warmed her. She'd been afraid he would deny her this right out of anger for her role in all this. But it seemed now, as they approached what would most likely be the most important battle in the history of their Tribe, he had forgiven her. That meant a great deal.

Of course, Khilai was not a Warrior. She had no training in martial combat, beyond the basic lessons every youngling learned, and she quickly discovered that she could help best by staying out of the way as Peraxis and his commanders organized the soldiers into their ranks. And what would she fight with, when the Danians came, she wondered. She had no weapons, no armor, and no Mugic. She had even left the Serpentotem behind. She was helpless!

Ah, but she had her claws, and her teeth, Khilai thought proudly. If she had to, she would scratch and bite at anyone who tried to get past her.

"Here." Someone thrust a spear at her, and Khilai accepted it reflexively, turning to identify her benefactor. Peraxis frowned and wouldn't meet her eye. "You might as well not make a fool out of yourself," the general muttered as he moved away. Khilai smiled and hefted her new weapon. Yes, she could use this. Not well, perhaps, but it was something.

Any further thoughts were interrupted as the ground shook beneath her feet.

"They're coming!" someone shouted, and all eyes turned toward the jungle beyond their border. Khilai tightened her grip on the spear, planting its butt in the sand between her feet and angling it so its gleaming tip pointed ahead of her and slightly upward. She was ready.

Her courage faltered, however, as the pounding and shaking increased, and then a shadow swept into view through the trees and vines. A shadow that was growing as it drew closer.

She felt her heart stutter as she realized it was no shadow. It was figures marching by the thousands. She had been right. The Danians were about to attack!

"Get ready!" Kehn-Sep's bellow broke the silence. She glanced toward him as his wings unfurled and he rose above their people, his sword catching and reflecting the sunlight until she could barely look at him. "We fight for our lives here, and our homes! We fight for Mipedim!"

"For Mipedim!" the soldiers shouted back. Khilai shouted with them.

The trees were swaying, bent aside, and the shadow rose, taking form. Now she could see individual heads and bodies and arms within it, grays and browns and blacks, with wide, faceted eyes set in triangular heads above. Then the shadow swept into the scrub brush, and they could clearly see the approaching Danians. She had never really believed there could be so many of them! All of them carried spears and swords and axes in their hands, many hefting more than one weapon, for they had four arms apiece. All of them had gleaming chitin, natural armor against Attack.

And all of them had glazed eyes that glowed faintly even in the sunlight.

"Attack!" Kehn-Sep commanded. The Danians were on the last length of dirt now, mere footsteps from the sand, and Khilai crouched down as the first of the soldiers reached her. One of them slammed into her spear and the impact threw her back a step, but she clenched her jaw and forced herself to push back even as it hacked at her.

The battle had begun.

For a time, Khilai saw and heard and knew nothing beyond her own struggle. That first Danian had fallen before her spear, but another had taken its place at once, and two more beside it. She stabbed and swung and blocked, her rage and fear substituting for skill; at least hefting a spear was similar to wielding her staff, only with a blade at the tip instead of a crystal. Khilai fought, and took cuts and scrapes and bruises, but she stayed standing throughout.

Then a Danian charged her, knocking her spear aside, its paired swords raised high to strike her down. Terrified, Khilai reacted instinctively. She flung out her hand and shouted, "Windslash!"

And stared, amazed, as a sharp wind drove the Danian from her, tumbling back into his fellows.

Khilai shook herself, unable to believe what had just happened. She had summoned the Air, and it had responded! Quickly she raised her hands and sang a tune to gather light, and almost cried as she saw the glow build around her fingers. Yes! It was weaker than it would have been just a few days before, but it was something!

And now she had a weapon far more potent than any spear.

Thinking of weapons reminded her—her staff! The Serpentotem had been leaning against a wall in her chambers when she'd felt the Mugic vanish, and she had left it there in her mad dash to the throne room. It must still be there! Closing her eyes, Khilai sang to it, summoning it across the distance, and smiled as she felt its familiar surface appear in her grip. She opened her eyes in time to see two more Danians about to strike her down, but a quick burst of light from the staff's eyes stunned them, and blows to their heads drove them to the ground instead.

She was the High Mugess once more.

Quickly she looked around. It was chaos. The Danians had been in perfectly ordered ranks but that had vanished when the two armies had met, and now there were clusters of fighting everywhere. Including, she was sorry to note, several where Mipedians fought Mipedians. That could only mean one thing.

The M'arrillians were here as well.

Khilai drew forth the orbs and selected a rosy red one, then tossed it high into the air. It hung there as she sent her spirit into it and called out, the orb's Hymn of Unity cascading across the sky. The Mugic wafted into the air, seeking those like her, and within minutes, she heard it answered from somewhere to her right. Another voice chimed in an instant later, and then two more. Their voices twined together, and Khilai directed the melody toward a spot off to one side and slightly behind the battle, a small dune where they would be able to see the conflict more clearly. As the Mugic settled there, she felt it tugging at her to follow, and gave in to its demands.

She vanished from the battlefield.

Khilai reappeared atop the dune in a burst of light and music. Others joined her, shimmering into existence as the melody summoned them: Firizon, Kirun, Shimo, and Ahila. The four Muges looked surprised, thrilled, even elated, and Khilai was sure her face bore the same mingled emotions.

"Our Mugic has returned!" Firizon shouted out of pure glee, the horrors below forgotten for just an instant in the wake of such wonderful news. Khilai smiled and joined in the general delight. She, too, felt like dancing and singing now that the music flowed once more through her veins.

But there wasn't time.

"It is weaker than it was," she pointed out, dampening their enthusiasm. "In fact, except for a few small tricks we can only draw upon it through the orbs. And we do not know how long it will last." She sighed and leaned on her staff. "We must make the most of its return, while we can."

The others nodded, properly chastened, and they all looked toward the battle. It was not going well. From here they could clearly see how badly their Warriors were outnumbered. In many places there were flashes of red, gold, green, and brown within the black and gray, flowing with that monochrome current as mind-controlled

Mipedians joined forces with the invading Danians. Then a flutter of gold caught her eye. A single figure rose above the tumult, wings spread, sword gleaming. Kehn-Sep!

But even as she watched, Khilai saw a streak of green race to answer the king's ascent. The M'arrillian swooped down like a hunting bird, its gaze sweeping across Kehn-Sep's face sharper than any talons. His wings faltered, and he dropped, but caught himself, his feet just scraping the head of a Danian. Then Kehn-Sep was flying alongside the M'arrillian, and Khilai's vision blurred with tears when she saw that the king was circling obediently behind the invader rather than attacking.

Their king had been taken. The battle was over.

There was only one hope left.

"We must stop the M'arrillians ourselves!" she urged her Muges. Unfortunately they were as shocked by their Tribe's defeat as she was, but she forced herself to go on. "If we can overpower the Fluidmorphers, we may be able to free our people from their control!"

"What about the Sphere?" Firizon demanded. "We were never able to defeat whoever held it."

Khilai nodded, heart and mind both racing. "True, but do you sense it here? Because I do not!"

She waited impatiently as the others cast about with mystic senses, but the hope and determination that grew on their faces was worth the delay.

"They must have left it behind for safekeeping," Ahila muttered. She clenched her hands into fists. "We have a chance!"

"Yes, but we have to act now, before they realize what we are doing," Khilai insisted. She pulled a smooth, sapphire blue crystal from her pouch. "We must sing a Song of Dismissal as we have never sung before!" She held out her staff, and the others grasped it as well, one by one. Then she raised the crystal high and released it to hang above their heads.

Khilai poured every ounce of Mugic she had left into the crystal, along with every scrap of will and every breath of focus, all channeled by anger and pain and fear and love. She was singing the song herself, though she knew the melody belonged to the crystal alone now. Yet singing it made her feel as if she were still the one shaping the Mugic. The others concentrated with her, their voices joined out of habit as well, and slowly the Mugic that poured from the crystal gathered and began to form a glowing, glittering net. Khilai struggled to keep her voice steady despite her growing jubilation. It was working! If they could make the net large enough, the song could drape across the entire battlefield, and free not only their own Tribe but the Danians as well! Then they would see how the M'arrillians fared against two Tribes out for blood and vengeance!

A shadow settled over her, and Khilai felt her scales prickle. Someone was hovering above them! It had to be a Fluidmorpher! She refused to stop or even glance up. She couldn't risk being dominated, not now. Then a familiar voice called her name, and she faltered despite herself.

"Khilai?"

She glanced up without thinking—and gaped, the melody fading as she temporarily forgot how to speak, much less sing or concentrate. A gold-scaled figure she knew all too well floated not two lengths away, close enough that she could have reached out and grabbed his foot.

Varakarr.

Her former apprentice gazed down upon her and his former fellow Muges. The song fell apart, the Mugic dissipating, as they all stared at him. None of them knew what to say. What was he doing here?

The question answered itself when a second figure appeared over Varakarr's shoulder. Khilai had only seen his image through Varakarr's magic, but she recognized the bulging fish eyes, wide lipless mouth, flat head, crestlike fin, and shoulder tentacles nonetheless. And

Firizon's wordless cry of rage only proved the Creature's identity.

M'ahadil. The Fluidmorpher who had—with Varakarr's help—stolen the Khilaian Sphere. The one who had given the M'arrillians the power to dominate the other Tribes. The architect of their downfall.

Khilai glared at him, matching him gaze for gaze—and realized too late her mistake. There was a burst of light, and she fought instinctively even as she felt her mental shields shatter under the onslaught. So strong! Then the Fluidmorpher's mind was wrapping around her own like a warm, thick blanket, shutting out all light and thought.

I can't let it end like this, Khilai thought desperately. Using the very last of her strength, she clasped the last orb she held, pouring her thoughts into the smoky gray orb as it warbled a Song of Translocation. She had no particular destination in mind, just the need to escape quickly. She felt the Mugic spin around her, whisking her away even as her senses dimmed. She had no idea where she would wind up, but anywhere was better than here!

"Excellent work, Varakarr," she heard M'ahadil say just before she vanished. "My thanks." Her rage at her former student's betrayal helped Khilai stay conscious long enough to be sure the song had worked. She was somewhere dark, a cave or cavern most likely, and well away from the battle.

Then, her last reserves depleted, she dropped to her knees, the song fading from her lips. After that, Khilai the High Mugess of Mipedim knew no more.

M'ahadil sighed with relief as the Mipedian Muges all straightened, their minds now under his control. That had been a close one! He had just arrived from Kaizeph in time to see the battle's end, and had spotted the Muges off to the side on their sand dune. He'd known at once they were planning something. He had flown over as fast as he could, the dominated Varakarr in tow, and had sensed the Mugic at work before he had seen the net of light and sound they were weaving. M'ahadil wasn't sure how it would affect those it touched, but had decided it was best not to find out.

The problem had been finding a way to distract the Muges from their task before they could finish. M'ahadil had known that showing himself would only fuel them to greater efforts. But their own friend and peer? That was another matter! He had sent Varakarr ahead of him, and had him call out to the High Mugess, and it had worked perfectly—the Muges had been so stunned, they'd lost their concentration. From there it had been an easy matter to dominate them one at a time.

It was a shame Khilai herself had escaped, but she was one Muge, all alone. She wouldn't pose a threat, especially not with the Mugic still so weak. Perhaps he'd hunt her down later.

And now it was over. Gathering the Muges to float behind him in a net of psionic force, M'ahadil swiveled to study the battlefield he had just passed. The last of the Mipedians had fallen to his fellow Fluidmorphers. And he had already heard from Teren'kar that the OverWorlders and UnderWorlders were theirs as well. The four Tribes were firmly under their control.

M'ahadil smiled as he began making his way back toward the Deep Ocean. The world of Perim was theirs. The M'arrillian Empire had begun.

The End